DAWG

Gladys Hill

authorHOUSE®

AuthorHouse™
1663 Liberty Drive
Bloomington, IN 47403
www.authorhouse.com
Phone: 1-800-839-8640

First published by AuthorHouse   1/24/2011

ISBN: 978-1-4567-3493-0 (sc)
ISBN: 978-1-4567-3494-7 (e)

Library of Congress Control Number: 2011906430

Printed in the United States of America

Dawg
--Was Pa's word (drawn out) for Dog

Author's Note

The shantyboys were important American Frontiersmen with a way of life individually their own. From all parts of the country they came to work the endless pines; from the East Coast to the rapidly advancing West they blazed the trails that led to expansion. It was their labor that birthed a giant industry and helped build a nation from the Atlantic to the Pacific.

Unlike the cowboys the shantyboys were not well publicized in song and story. Minimal credit has been given their contribution as they traveled up and down and across the wilderness, hacking, chopping, skidding, hauling, riding the great pine logs that fed the saws for a giant industry. Their labors were as significant to the development of the North as the cowboys' role was in the development of the West.

My grandfather was a shantyboy, so called because they lived in shanties in the woods. Grandpa was born in 1861. During the early 1880's he guided his team of slow moving oxen from his home in Columbia County, to the pineries of Northern Wisconsin. Butternut, Park Falls, Fosterville (now Presque Isle), Sayner and Star Lake were areas mentioned. There he lived the life of a shantyboy all winter; in the spring he returned to his farm in Southern Wisconsin with cash in his pockets.

From Grandpa I learned of the shantyboys, of their influence and their importance to the economy. Theirs was a strong and vital endowment to America.

Prologue

The team of dun—colored oxen, still hitched to the high-wheeled ox cart, patiently chewed their cuds. Occasionally one stamped a foot or switched his tail at an annoying early spring insect. The now empty cart had been heaped high with wood, but Big Jim Stewart had made swift work of that. A neat stack of hickory, oak, and maple chunks stood near the front entrance to the tidy white farmhouse, nearly hidden by clustering evergreens and scattered maples with still furled leaves of pale spring green. The split hardwood was heaped on the back porch, close to the kitchen door.

"Guess that'll hold us for awhile."

Big Jim good—naturedly slapped the rump of the off ox and started up the steps to the kitchen.

"Mary," he called. "Think that'll do you so's you can bake up one of those special pie—plant pies? I sure got a hankering for a home baked rhubarb pie. There's quite a lot of stalks, nice and red, over in the garden, just waiting to be baked up in a nice crusty, juicy pie." Without waiting for an answer he added, "You'd better get me some good old farmer clothes. These wool duds are too darn hot for this weather."

Jim Stewart was big, dark, and swarthy, and looked especially rugged dressed in a red and black wool shirt, stagged woolen trousers, and stout leather boots, standard garb of a lumberjack fresh from the pinery of northern Wisconsin. His thick black hair hung nearly to his shoulders. He passed a hand across his beard reflectively as he rubbed his jaw.

"While you're at it, get the scissors, too. This hair'n beard's gotta go."

A slight, fair, blue—eyed woman appeared in the kitchen doorway. Although she was dressed in a somber long gray dress of the mid 1880s, her clothing did not completely conceal her physical comeliness. The brightness of her smile crinkled the corners of her eyelids and belied the soberness of her garb.

"Take off your shirt," she commanded, and raised her hand above her eyebrow in a half salute, and also to shade her eyes from the brilliant spring sunlight. "I'll get the shears for you, sir." She laughed happily. "It'll be a pleasure to relieve you of all that wool. We'll do this little chore right here on the stoop and keep the hair out of my kitchen. Looks to me like there'll be enough hair this time for Gramma to make a hair pillow."

Jim joined in her laughter. "I'd best shed this wool undershirt or I'll end up wearing a hair shirt, and Lord knows I'm not a monk about to chastise myself for my iniquities."

He took her in his arms and held her close. "Mary, sweet Mary," he murmured tenderly. "It's so good to be home. So good to be with you. I miss you so much, so very, very much." He stroked her face tenderly, outlining each feature with his finger. "Winters are so long. I do miss you so much."

Even before Jim and Mary were married, (fifteen years come May), Big Jim had left his home in central Wisconsin each fall and worked in the pineries, way up north, Sayner, Park Falls, Butternut, Buswell, Fosterville.

He was wont to say, "When I first went to the pinery I thought those big pines would last forever. We believed the timber would never end and we could always cut the big pines. We cut the best and let the rest lay. You could smell the rosin and pine chips for miles before you reached the woods. On a hot day you could catch a good whiff of the pinery on the evening breeze here on the farm. Made a fellow feel close, somehow. That was before the fires began. Late years it's been pine smoke I'm smelling on a hot, dry summer wind, and that's bad news . . . for man and beast."

In later years Jim had his own team of oxen to work in the woods, those dun—colored beasts that waited so patiently under the heavy yoke. All winter he lived the life of a shantyboy, cutting the timber, icing roads, hauling logs, decking logs. It was difficult and dangerous work, and a man looked death in the face every day. Accidents were frequent, but a man got- used to the danger, and Big Jim was careful; he had a lot to live for.

When the break—up came, with the warm spring breezes and melting snow and ice, logs were rafted down the various streams and rivers to the big mills and sawed into lumber for houses, barns, and factories. Big Jim never rode the rafts; he collected his pay and started the long trek home. He would be home, usually in early April, and have plenty of time to till the fields and plant his crops.

Big Jim knew exactly what he would do with this past winter's wages. He would be able to make the final payment on the farm, and still have a few dollars cash money. Cash money was scarce and a dollar had immense buying power. He had had his share of bad farming years, but now things were looking up.

"Just one more year in the woods," he gloated to himself. "Next year I'll be able to put most of the cash in the bank for a rainy day. We'll fix up the house some, too. Put in a cistern and a pitcher pump by the sink, so Mary won't have to haul water from the creek when she washes clothes and the kids take baths."

The road home had seemed shorter behind those slow—moving oxen when he thought about the future and made plans for his family. There was Mary, his loving helpmate; he hated the leave—taking in the fall, but he would not think about that now. There were the children, Johnny, his firstborn, named after Pa but dark and swarthy like himself; and towheaded Little Jim, his namesake, but who was slight and fair like Mary; Baby Inga—-he could almost feel those pudgy little hands pulling his beard and hear her joyful laughter when he grabbed her and tossed her in his arms.

"More, more," she would cry. "Do it some more, Pa."

"Ingie's going on four. She really ain't a baby anymore," he said, and he felt a pang of sadness. "They grow up so fast. I miss being there with them. But one more winter and I'll be home for good."

He thought tenderly of his active little mother, Ingaborg. She was of sturdy Scandinavian stock, industrious and energetic, always doing something, a doer, a goer, and a giver. As for his horse—loving father, how he depended on him to see that everything was well and going good for Mary and the kids. They were Gramma and Grampa to the kids. Good friends, the neighbors described them. Oh, he would be glad to get home, and so welcome.

Once he reached home, Jim could not wait to shed the trappings of the woods, along with his long hair and curly black beard. He became busily engaged in the affairs of the farm; it was as though he had never been away.

The farm in spring was such a beautiful, busy place, with new life bursting forth wherever you looked. The wee baby leaves of spring green fluttered against the vivid blue Wisconsin sky, and spring was a gossamer veil tossed over the new growth of the pines and the stark nakedness of the hardwoods.

"There's wood aplenty to last us all summer," Big Jim said, pointing. "I'll put the beasts in the pasture'n you can get my clothes ready. Hope you've got plenty of hot water in the range reservoir, 'cause I'm going to need a bath after I shed this hair."

Jim tugged at his beard. "I feel like a buffalo with all this fur around my face. Can't wait to get rid of it. I know I'll itch worse'n a dog with fleas, but it's too early to jump in the creek yet. When I come up from pasturing the animals I'll tote a couple buckets of water to get warm on top of the stove. They'll heat up by the time you get me trimmed."

It had been a sad glad—homecoming that year, and it had taken longer to get in the swing of things. Grandpa Stewart, (Honest John to his friends and neighbors), was laid to rest nearly a month before Big Jim made it home.

Gramma was staying with Mary and the children, and the family had had time to adjust somewhat to their loss, but it had been a bad time for Jim this spring. He was just beginning to get a hold on things these past few days.

The week after Jim came home, Gramma moved Baby Ingie into the spare room downstairs with her. "I need the company and she's getting too big to be sleeping with you and Mary. You can't get your rest, three in a bed."

So it was settled. Gramma and Ingie would share the spare room, and the spare room became Gramma and Ingie's room.

Too, it was settled after long hours of debate that Big Jim would go to the pinery one more year.

"Johnny is such a responsible boy, and almost a man these days," Gramma said. "Got more sense'n some men. You should see how he took hold when Grandpa died, good as any grown—up man. 'Sides, the farm work's all done before you leave, it's only regular chores all winter. And you know Cousin Jerry's right next door and he'll look in on us. We'll get along just fine."

They were brave women folk, Gramma, and his Mary. Johnny was convincing, too. "I can do it, Pa. I know I can. Give me a chance."

The rest is Johnny's story.

Chapter 1

The kitchen door flew open and Ma burst out on the stoop. "Whatever is going on here?" she demanded, having to yell to make herself heard.

I said, "Little Jimmy dragged this old, moth—eaten dog home from school."

"He's my dog," Jimmy insisted. "He is so. I'm agonna keep him. Them kids was mean, throwin' stones and hitting him with sticks. He's mine." Then he put his face right beside that mean looking, ugly dog's face.

"Be careful!" I shouted in alarm. "He might bite you."

That mangy cur knew I didn't trust him and he flattened out on the ground like he would bury himself right down deep. He looked up at me with sad, soft brown eyes, his tail twitching just a little.

I reached down and grabbed him by the scruff of the neck, and he began to yelp, the loudest, most blood-curdling yelps you ever did hear from an animal. That set Little Jim going, and he began to scream and yell and kick and fistfight, worse than a wildcat.

"You're hurting my dog! Stop hurting my dog!" he yelled fiercely.

Pa came hurrying around the side of the barn. "What in Sam Hill is all this ruckus about?" He had to holler, too, to make himself heard.

"Little Jim dragged this ugly mutt home," I said. "The minute I touched him, he began to yelp his fool head off. You'd think I was killing him."

I gave that old dog a dirty look and he began to whimper and grovel on the ground, and look sad and crawl on his belly. He was the ugliest, stupidest, most unnecessary piece of dog flesh I'd ever seen. He had a homely, hairy face and a long, skinny tail. His ribs stuck out, and he had a flea—bit hide with fur coming off in patches so he looked spotty all over.

"I don't trust him," I said. "He looks worse'n the wolf in Ingie's Little E Riding Hood book. I'll get rid of him. I can chase him down the road a piece."

That dumb dog seemed to know what I said, because he kept crawling on his belly, ending right up in front of Pa and looking up with those sad eyes, begginglike.

"Just look at him," I said in disgust. "You can tell he's no—account, crawling on his belly that way."

Little Jimmy had quit bawling but tears were running down his cheeks.

"Please, Pa. He's a good dog. Can I have him, Pa? Will you let me keep him? Please, Pa."

I walked away in disgust and turned my back on the whole dumb show.

Pa said, "Take 'er easy, John. We'll let him stay a few days. He ain't much of a dog, but I hate secin' critters go hungry. Little Jim can haul some clean straw and make him a bed in the corner of the barn. Ma'll find something for him to eat."

Little Jim quit bellering, and Pa bent over and petted the cur. "Good old boy. Good dog."

That big lummox rolled over and over, his big feet flapping the air and his tail pounding the stoop like a hammer.

"C'mon now, Dawg," Little Jim said, imitating the way Pa drawled the word "dog."

Dawg now had a name. He stood up and stretched, wagging his tale just a little.

Pa spoke softly. "That old dog ain't got the look of a mean dog. We could use him. Give him a chance, Johnny boy. Maybe he'll be real good around here. We need a dog since old Brownie's gone."

Good old Brownie; he'd fought with two big boar coons that were raiding Ma's garden. Brownie was hurt so bad, Pa had to shoot him. Gramma was real good at fixing hurt animals, but this time there wasn't anything she could do, except tell Pa, "Do it quick. Put him out of his misery."

Pa shot the big male that Brownie had been fighting. Brownie had killed the other one.

Pa said, "This one would have died, too, but I couldn't leave it to crawl off somewhere and suffer. Brownie'd have done all right with just one of those boars. Two of 'em was too much for even Brownie to handle."

I said, "Ain't no other dog can take Brownie's place: Not for me, there ain't."

Pa nodded his head in agreement. "Of course not, son. Brownie'll always have a special place in your heart. Mine, too. We'll all remember him, but he was mostly your dog. You'll miss him lots, but this will be a good dog, maybe. We'll see. He's been used pretty bad and kept tied. Just see where the hair is all worn away on his neck. That rope or chain was too tight for him. Just pet him . . . , there's welts and scars all over his body. Some of 'em might come from fighting, but someone has treated him mighty bad."

Now, at night, as soon as we got home from school, Jimmy would run and get fresh straw for Dawg to sleep in. He took the currycomb from the stable and combed and curried that flea—bitten mutt until patches of hair came out.

Dawg would stretch out full length on the green grass and lie still, except for his head turning first one way and then the other, his mouth wide open and that long red tongue lolling out. Little Jim would yank and pull and comb handsful of fuzzy brown—black hair off Dawg's back and legs and belly. Dawg loved all that attention. He'd let Ingie sit on him and poke and pull at him, too.

The good food Ma was giving him helped. His ribs didn't stick out anymore and his coat began to shine and his fur was thick and soft. When Ma came out and petted him he'd nearly turn inside out. Jimmy would yell and scream, telling him to stay still so he could comb him.

Ma would just say, "Lie still, Dawg. Be good for Jimmy," and he'd quiet right down, just his tail wagging.

That fool dog tagged Ma everywhere. When he was in the house he followed her from room to room. If she went to the window and looked out, he stood on his hind legs and looked out. If she walked to the door, he was right behind her. If she went to the well for a bucket of water, or to work in her garden, or in the barn, Dawg stayed close by. If she stood by the railing on the front porch talking to one of us, Dawg stood on his hind legs beside her. He'd look first at her and then at the other person, pretending he understood what was going on.

Dawg liked being in the house during the day, because he'd push the door open and go out when he liked, but at night he wanted out. He didn't sleep in the barn anymore, no matter how good a bed he had there. He'd lie stretched out on the stoop, watching. If the weather was bad, and it was raining, he crawled underneath the stoop, ready to bark and put the run on any intruder.

"He's a real good watch dog," Pa said.

"He's a real dumb dog," I said. "Watch him chase his tail."

Around and around in a circle that dog chased his tail. He'd whirl around so fast, the dust flew up in clouds and all you'd see was a whirling blackish brown blur in the center of a cloud of dust.

Gramma stood on the stoop and watched. "His body's lacking something it needs," she said. "The good food he's getting now is helping him. Maybe an egg every couple of days would be good for him."

Little Jim heard what Gramma said and dashed for the chicken house.

"My dog needs an egg," he yelled, and came back with one still warm from the chicken. He would have fed it to Dawg, shell and all, but Pa said, "Maybe you'd better crack it open."

Old Dawg really smacked his lips on that one. Jimmy saw to it that Dawg had an egg every day.

A couple weeks went by.

One night at supper Ma said, "Something's getting the eggs out of the chicken coop. I'm hardly getting enough for us to eat. I thought maybe the hens were stealing their nests so I kept them fenced in, but that hasn't helped. They should be laying good right now."

Pa said, "It can't be a mink or a weasel. They'd kill the chickens. With all these cats and Dawg, I don't think there's any rats around, but we'll keep watch."

Next noonday, I'd just finished carrying the slops to Porkie and was standing by the pigpen, scratching Corkie's back. Dawg came loping down the path and hopped that chicken yard fence like it was a foot high, and tail wagging like an old lady's tongue, he slipped into the chicken house.

Big Red, Ma's big Rhode Island Red rooster, had his harem safe in one corner of the yard. He was raising a ruckus, cackling and strutting stiff—legged, but he didn't challenge Dawg. I ran through the gate, and there was Dawg, gobbling every egg left in the nests.

"Why, you thieving cur," I yelled. "No wonder you look so shiny and glossy." He must have had a dozen eggs. "Everybody braggin' you up and you're just nothin' but an old egg sucker."

I had to tell Ma and yet I hesitated. Ma would be mad, that's for sure. You know, by now I'd kind of half liked that big ugly mutt. He'd slip up beside me and stick that cold nose of his into my hand, and sort of nuzzle me like he liked me.

I yelled, "Dawg! You dirty thief. Come here!"

He was always happy with any attention, but he sort of hung back and cringed when he came. He followed me up to the house, coming along when I called, but sort of lagging back, too.

I said, "Ma, here's the thief. This dog is nothing but an egg-stealing mongrel, not worth his salt."

Dawg looked brow—beaten and his tail barely wiggled, but he looked up at me with the saddest look, and stuck his nose up close and licked my hand with that long old tongue of his.

I could see that Ma felt bad—-Gramma, too. Pa'd been resting a few minutes before going back in the field. He came outside; he looked sad and sorry.

"We can't keep him if he's an egg sucker," he said. "I'll get rid of him after supper. Sure do hate to do it. Little Jim'll take it mighty hard. He sets such store on that dog," and Pa motioned to me to keep quiet.

Little Jim had been listening in the doorway. He came after me with both fists and feet, yelling and bawling.

"Dawg never is a thief. He's my dog. You made that up 'cause you don't like him."

Jimmy ran to Pa. "Please, please don't hurt Dawg. He's a good dog. John doesn't like him, that's what," and he picked up a handful of rocks and began pelting me.

Ingie was bawling, too. I felt as though I was the thief. I didn't want to see that dog put away, but I'd caught him red-handed. Something had to be done.

Gramma spoke up. "For heaven's sake. What's all this fuss about?"

I started to say something but she *ssh—shed* me.

"All this noise about a dog sucking a few eggs. Well, I never! That's easy to fix. We'll just break him from that little habit."

"How?"

"Can you?" We all wanted to know.

Gramma was a regular wizard when it came to home remedies. She knew which herbs and weeds to pick for medicinal purposes and what to do for frostbite or sunburn or chilblains; she believed in sulphur and molasses for spring doldrums and sulphur and lard for the itch. She picked dandelion greens, and fiddlehead ferns and the young cowslips, besides nettles and lots of different kinds of mushrooms——all good for you after a long cold winter.

Gramma knew someone who would buy your warts so they'd fall off in a couple weeks, and someone else owned a madstone that could cure hydrophobia. A madstone is very rare. It comes from the stomach of a deer or cow or goat. You place the stone on the bite or sore where it sticks. When it falls off it is full of poison and must be soaked in milk to remove the poison before you put it back on the sore.

Gramma gave directions. "In the morning we'll pick the eggs early. Hens have 'most finished laying by noon. We'll keep Dawg in the house, if we have to tie him. Then John can put this egg I fix up in one of the nests. Then let Dawg out. If he gets the right egg, it'll cure him!"

Gramma checked her collection for cayenne. She mixed two parts cayenne pepper and one part soda. Then she warmed beeswax and patted it real thin, and formed it around a spoon. Next, she rolled it around the cayenne mixture. There was a little hole on top and she melted beeswax to seal it. Then she put it in a cool place till morning.

The next day I picked the eggs and checked again for eggs before we let Dawg out of the house. Gramma took one of the eggs that was still warm, made a small hole in it and let some of the white dribble out. Then she worked the capsule of cayenne she'd concocted in the hole and pushed some egg shell from another egg over it; the egg white made the piece of shell stick to the egg.

"Now take it out and put it in one of the nests," she said. "When Dawg bites into that he'll know he's got a mouthful."

I came back to the house, and before we let him out, Gramma gave him a bowl of warm milk. We watched. Dawg pretended to be real innocent and smelled around the trees. He checked on the pigs and ran in the stable and came out sniffing like he was looking for something. When he didn't see anyone around, he trotted up the path and made one flying leap into the chicken yard.

As usual, Big Red herded the hens over in one corner and Dawg trotted into the henhouse like he owned it. We heard one yelp and Dawg came hightailing it through the henhouse door. In one bound Dawg made it over the fence and headed straight for the creek, his mouth wide open. There was white foam around his lips and dripping from his tongue.

What happened next was a sight to behold. Dawg was making long, flying leaps, his ears flapping, his mouth and tongue slavering white foam; his tail was between his legs, so tight you didn't think he had a tail. He dashed pell—mell into the creek.

It all happened so fast, in less time than it takes to tell it, Dawg dove into the deepest water, gulping and slurping in great mouthfuls.

"He's got the fits," Ma cried.

Gramma said, "That was one hot egg. He's just trying to get rid of the hot stuff."

Dawg wasn't done yet. We were glued to the ground where we stood. Anything a dog ever did, he did, besides some things I never saw a dog do. He rolled. He slid. He spun. He did somersaults and headstands, in the water, out of the water. He gyrated like a top spinning out of control.

At last, his tail hanging limp and his sides heaving convulsively, he stood on the bank and gagged, bringing up the loathsome egg.

Gramma looked at me. "He'll be fine now." To Ma she said, "That was soda bubbling with his saliva. Looked awful, didn't it? But it soothes his innards——that's why I gave him milk. We'll give him some more warm milk now. It coats his insides and takes away the burning. He'll be top dog again tomorrow.

You'll see. Bet you that old fool won't be so anxious to eat eggs from now on."

Gramma was right. Dawg shied clear of the henhouse. If anyone offered him an egg, he'd assume a hangdog expression, stick his tail between his legs and slink away.

Chapter 2

Ingie was celebrating her fourth birthday that spring. Ingie's name was really Inga; she was named after Gramma, whose name was Ingaborg.

When Pa saw that wee little girl, he said, "That's too much name for a little mite like that to carry around—-we'll call her Inga."

Gramma agreed. "I didn't know my name was Ingaborg until I was twenty," she said, and laughed. "My pa was a Welshman and he and my uncles and my brothers called me Lassie. So did my ma, most of the time. Once I married your father and I started having children, Lassie sounded pretty silly for a grown—up woman. So they began calling me Inga. Still do."

Gramma was Pa's mother, and his family was great on using the same names over and over. I was John, after my grandpa and his grandpa; Little Jim was James, after Pa and his uncles and Pa's grandfather. There were Johns and Jims in every Stewart family from way back.

Grandpa said, "We've got to keep the Norwegian names in the family, too," so Baby Ingie was christened Inga.

Her fourth birthday was kind of glad and sad, both, for all of us. This was the first birthday in the family since Grandpa died. We missed him. He was always teasing and laughing and full of fun. It just wasn't the same without him, and for sure Gramma missed him most of all. She didn't cry, but tears were in her eyes a couple times that day.

Gramma and Grandpa had lived close by. In fact, Pa's farm had been part of Grandpa's, but when the railroad came through it had cut the farm in two. Grandpa kept the north side of the tracks and we were on the south side.

The day Grandpa died he'd been breaking a lively young riding horse. After the funeral Gramma came to live with us. She said keeping busy and having young'uns around kept her from being too sad.

Gramma had made a little red pocketbook for Ingie and decorated it with white beadwork. Ma had driven Old Joe to the store and bought some bright calico with little flowers all over. She and Gramma made Ingie a pinafore. Pa bought stick candy so we could each have one, but Ingie had two in a little brown paper bag. In the bottom of the bag Ma put a tiny cake of maple sugar with fluted edges.

We had lots of maple trees on the farm. Every spring we gathered the sap from the sugar bush, Grandpa Dawg called it. Besides sugar and syrup, Ma always made some tiny cakes of pure maple sugar for special occasions.

Ingie was so happy all dressed up in her new pinafore. Ma

had saved a strip of the same material, and she tied a perky little bow in Ingie's top hair. Ingie looked like a big doll, all pink and white, with curly blonde hair.

"Can I go out and show Mrs. Murphy how I look?" Ingie asked.

She and Little Jim played with the farm animals and gave them names. A calf, a litter of kittens, baby pigs, all were important events and duly named. Timothy and Tom were the team of oxen. Old Joe was Ma's buggy horse. Porkie and Corkie, the pigs, and the cows were Spot and Blackie. Mrs. Smith, Miss Cora and Mrs. Murphy were members of Big Red's harem; Big Red was an enormous rooster, mean and feisty. He chased the cats, Fluffy and Furry and Fanny and Oscar; he'd even put the run on good old Brownie, but that was because Brownie let him. Brownie knew he was part of the farm.

When Big Red got too cocky Pa'd douse him with a bucket of cold water and threaten, "You watch out or it's the soup kettle for you."

Big Red kept a good watch for hawks and varmints and protected the hens.

Ma said, "Ingie, baby, leave your new purse in here so you don't soil it. Hang onto your bag with the candy, don't drop it in the dirt."

Ingie bounced out the door and into the yard. "Mrs. Murphy, Mrs. Murphy, come and see." She opened her bag, and holding it in front of her, squatted down. "Just see what I've got, Mrs. Murphy." Ingie opened her bag wider. "I'm four years old today. Just look at me."

She preened herself and chattered constantly. The old hen

cocked her head to one side as she cackled softly. Sedately, she stepped up to peer in the bag.

Suddenly Mrs. Murphy's head shot forward, she snatched the bag in her beak and ran for the chicken coop. Ingie wailed, jumped to her feet, and began the chase. Shouting and crying, her face red and angry, her short legs flew over the ground.

Another hen ran up, snatched the paper bag and took off in a different direction. Big Red decided to get into the act. He cocked his head, flapped his wings, and with long, running strides he soon had the prize. Ingie collapsed into a small sniveling heap, crying softly.

Dawg went into action. There was a flurry of dust, red feathers flew, and Dawg had the bag. Head high, he ran over to Ingie and gently dropped the brown bag in front of her, his long tail doing flip—flops from side to side. Ingie's recovery was miraculous. She hopped to her feet and threw both arms around Dawg, giving him a regular bear hug.

Dawg lapped up all the praise and petting and attention like a cat slurping cream. He'd lost his hangdog expression long since, and he now assumed a cocky, alert I'm—right--on—the—job look.

Ma worked in her garden nearly every morning before the sun was too hot. In the afternoon she and Gramma canned and churned or did countless household chores.

Ma hated snakes. There were lots of them around. Some crawled up the trees in the orchard and stole the eggs or ate the baby birds if they had hatched. Whenever we heard the birds making a big fuss in the orchard or in the bushes that grew alongside the stone fence, Pa would come and kill the snake.

There were spotted adders, pine snakes, blue racers, copperheads, and once in a while a rattlesnake from the swale would be coiled in the long dead grass in the orchard.

We had an outside cellar door, the kind you can slide down. There was a small space where the two doors overlapped, and sometimes a snake would crawl in there. When you lifted the cellar door you would hear a plop! and there would be a snake on the stone steps to the cellar. Ma never let the little ones go to the cellar by themselves, and before they played on the cellar door she checked to make sure there weren't any snakes.

After Dawg came she never had to worry. Pa believed keeping lots of cats kept the snakes away, but it was Dawg that really took care of the snakes.

Ma couldn't help herself when she saw a snake. She just yelled and shivered and shook all over. When Dawg heard Ma cry out, he'd come on the run. Then he'd hunt through the grass or brush until he located the snake, grab it in his mouth and shake it until it was almost dead, then he'd drop it on the ground and jump on it. He literally clawed the snakes to pieces.

Ma was afraid he'd be bitten, but like Pa said, "That old dog knows what he's doing. He's just too quick for 'em."

One afternoon, Ma was canning and Gramma was picking over berries, when Ingie woke up from her nap and wanted to play outdoors.

Ma, like always, said, "All right but stay close to the house."

Ingie played on the stoop with the cats for awhile. Then she saw a butterfly and started after it as it fluttered first one way and then the other. She couldn't catch it, but then she saw a little rabbit take off toward the creek.

"Bunny, bunny," she called. "Wait for Ingie."

Laughing and clapping her hands, she skipped and hopped, imitating the rabbit. Dawg ran along beside her, trying to head her back toward the house, but Ingie had made up her mind where she wanted to go. She kept dodging him, working her way closer to the water all the time.

Dawg grabbed the hem of her dress and held on while Ingie tugged and pulled and then began to cry. When she found she was cornered and couldn't get away she began to bawl and scream in earnest.

"Mama, Mama! Dawg is mean. Mean old, old dog."

She kicked and screamed at the top of her lungs. Dawg could only grr—r-r! because he couldn't open his mouth to bark and he wouldn't let go of Ingie's dress.

Ma heard the crying and came on the run. Ingie was a good quarter of a mile from the house and right near the edge of the creek where the water ran close to the bank, deep and swift.

Ingie said, through her tears, "I was just following the bunny hop-it, and Dawg wouldn't let me catch it."

Ma patted Dawg's head and hugged him. "Good old Dawg!"

Chapter 3

Neighbors were far apart. We didn't have company often, nor did we do much visiting. There was always a big celebration on Memorial Day and Independence Day; we all went to town those days. It was a good chance to see our neighbors, and almost all of our friends would be there.

The Fourth turned out to be a beautiful day, sunny and clear and not too hot, like it sometimes was that time of year.

Gramma was sad that day, although she tried not to show it. Grandpa'd always led the parade, mounted on his big black stallion, but this year Grandpa's cousin Jerimiah (Jerry) headed the parade, riding Lady. Lady was the filly Grandpa had been breaking the day he died. She was such a pretty, high—stepping little mare.

"Grandpa'd be real proud of her," Gramma said with a sigh.

"He surely loved his horses. If he'd just rested after riding her 'stead of going right to work on Black Roy, putting him through his paces, your grandpa'd most likely be here today. But he was bound that horse had to have exercise."

Black Roy was Grandpa's big black stallion, cantankerous and headstrong. When Grandpa had mounted him, Black Roy took the bit between his teeth and ran more than a mile, with Grandpa fighting him all the way. Finally Grandpa got the stallion turned and rode him back to the stable without any trouble, but working with Lady and the extra exertion needed to control Black Roy was too much.

When Grandpa came in the house he said, "I'm plumb tuckered out. I'm just too tired to eat," and he went to bed without eating supper. He told Gramma, bragging a little, "Guess I showed that old boy who's still the boss around here."

During the night Grandpa just slept away.

Gramma sold Black Roy right afterwards but she hadn't sold the farm yet, although she talked about it from time to time. Cousin Jerry was doing a good job running it, and he was taking good care of Grandpa's horses, and like Gramma said, "Keeps him busy. He's better off with something to do."

People came from all over to buy Grandpa's horses. They were part Arabian, lightweight and bred for riding or pulling a light buggy.

When Ma and Pa went to farming Grandpa had quit doing the heavy work. He sold Pa his team of oxen, and Grandpa just raised a few light crops, like oats and hay for the horses. He let the rest of his land revert to pasture for them.

When the parade was over, Cousin Jerry and his family joined us for a picnic lunch. We had cold fried chicken, baked beans, salad and pies. Jerry couldn't get over how well Lady behaved in the parade.

"Gentle as a kitten," he said, taking a big bite of a fried chicken leg. "She didn't pay no 'tention to that band playing or the veterans marching with their drums and bugles. The noisy crowd didn't faze her and she hardly flinched at all the firecrackers going off almost beside her."

"Those boys in blue sure stepped lively," Pa said. "Some of them are getting along in years. That's a long haul from the cemetery to the Baptist church."

On Memorial Day the parade ended at the cemetery and everyone visited the graves and put flowers and flags on the soldiers' graves, and services were held at the cemetery.

Since this was the Fourth, the parade started at the cemetery gate. The gate was a big grilled black iron gate, with Ohio Cemetery spelled across the top in big letters.

I'd asked Gramma, "Why does it say Ohio Cemetery?"

"Well, Johnny, it's kind of a long story, but there's a reason for it. You see, some early settlers in this part of the country migrated here from Ohio… like Grandpa and I came from Pennsylvania. These folks called their settlement Ohio, and that's what they named their cemetery.

"Later on, they wanted a post office here, and Matt Adams filled out the forms. He wrote real fancy, lots of flourishes and not too plain. Someone in the postmaster general's office thought the fancy O H written together was an R, and wrote it up as Rio. If Matt'd printed the word, the town'd be Ohio today. The gate cost so much money, the cemetery association figured just leave it———so the parade is from the Ohio Cemetery to the Rio Baptist Church."

I said, "The church sure looks different than on Sundays, all decorated up and so many people around it. I'll just bet Preacher Doud would be happy to see this many on Sunday."

"It makes a good meeting place," Cousin Jerry said. "I was sure glad I was riding Lady. Lots easier than marching all that ways. Besides, my old uniform is getting kinda tight. If I start hiking and sweating, I could bust my britches."

We all laughed at his sally.

Then he asked, "Did you see the Indians marching at the head of our boys? Some Indians have set up a camp at the forks on Duck Creek———that's Sam White's land. Sam's part Indian himself. Well, he found out that a couple of them braves had been in our division . . . talked 'em right into marching with us."

We gathered to listen to the speaker, who stood on the church steps so we could all hear. He was long—winded, but when he began talking about the railroads and saying that 'very soon we would have both the Northwestern and the Milwaukee Road just a few miles apart, everyone took notice. Last of all, he issued a warning:

"There's a counterfeit gang passing counterfeit money, and the government thinks it's coming from somewhere close to this area. So be on the watch. It's ten—dollar bills they're passing. If you get one, or know of anyone that might be passing them, get in touch with me. I'll never tell who told me."

I was glad when we all stood up to sing. We sang "Columbia,""The Blue and the Gray,""John Brown's Body,""The

Dying Wisconsin Soldier," "The Old Rugged Cross," and last of all, "The Star—Spangled Banner."

There were games and races, contests and ball games. I stayed with Pa and the other men while they talked crops and livestock and about how dry it was getting. They welcomed the news of the expanding railroad service, and the conversation veered to the counterfeiters. Cousin Jerry and some of the men figured they had a good idea where the bills were coming from.

"He gets on the train right here in town and heads for the big cities, Milwaukee and Chicago. Sometimes heads the other way, Minneapolis and St. Paul."

"Frank comes back here a different way every time. Never gets off at the same town twice, in case government agents are watching. He hikes back there in the swamp and he and Old Amos make another batch. Heard tell he makes the trip once a month."

"I saw him get off at the water tower once, when the engine took on water before making the grade. He knew what he was doing, just rolled down the bank and disappeared."

Another volunteered, "I hear tell Old Amos got plates that are pretty near perfect. Government man said his bills were almost impossible to tell from the real thing."

I was fascinated with the conversation, and asked, "Where does Old Amos live? Can't anybody find him or go see him? I never did see him, but I did see Frank, that other guy."

"Don't you ever try finding him," one man warned. "He's, a strange one, and he knows them swamps like the back of his hand. Heard him say once, 'If I catch anybody snooping around my place, I know a deep hole back yonder what nothin' ever comes up outta, and he meant it. He was talking about revenuers that time. He's got a still back there somewhere, too."

Pa spoke up. "Well, if it's true, they'll get caught sooner or later. The government isn't going to let something like making money go on forever. I can see not paying too much attention to a few batches of white mule, but if there's counterfeiting going on it's a different story."

Little Jim came running up, all out of breath, his blue eyes shinIng, excited because he won the sack race.

"I beated them big kids in that old bag race," he said, "but that little Indian boy beated all of us in a real race. Whew! could he ever run! I ran faster'n anything but I couldn't catch him."

Jimmy's blond hair was darkly wet and sweat was running down his red face, but he was grinning all over, hopping up and down, first on one foot and then the other.

"That's just great, but your face is dirty," I said. "That little Indian kid must've stirred up a lot of dust. You better go over by the pump and wash up 'fore Ma sees you."

Little Jim was a sight. Ma had even made me polish his shoes, and he fairly sparkled when we left home, his hair all slicked down and parted even, his shirt white and starchy and his pants creased.

Pa brushed the dust off Jimmy's pants. He took out his clean white handkerchief and wiped Jimmy's hair and face and neck, shook it out, took a rueful look at it, then used it to wipe Little Jim's scuffed shoes before he stuffed it down deep in his hip pocket.

"Sit down here and cool off before you go over to the pump. Are the games over yet?" he asked.

Cousin Jerry said, "You know, that little Indian kid must be from the Indian camp at the Forks. They're Winnebagos. Most of 'em are mighty good Indians, tend to their own business, don't bother nobody, but every once in a while there's a couple bad 'uns. Just like white folks. I recollect what fighters them Indians was in the War Between the States. There was Winnebagos and Chippewas in our regiment. We was glad to have them with us, on our side. And them braves'd follow Old Abe through the gates of hell and back again. Yes, sir, they was real good fighters, 'nd real good to have with you in a fight."

"Who was Old Abe?" I asked.

Little Jim was sitting tight to Pa, wide—eyed and quiet for once. Guess I was just as taken up.

"Never hear tell of Old Abe? Well, I'll tell you," Jerry continued. "A couple young bucks from Flambeau captured this baby eagle and tamed him. They brought him along to camp, and he became our mascot for the regiment. You never did see nothing like that. When we went into battle Old Abe flew high above us, flapping his wings, always just ahead of the men like he was leading us on, screaming, soaring, swooping. When the smoke got thick and there was shells bursting all 'round, Old Abe just kept right with us, screaming and screeching, flapping his wings just over our heads, leading the troops, screaming louder than the rifles.

"Fellers from the South put a bounty on his head—- they sure wanted that bird bad. Figured if they got him outta the way, we'd lose our courage.

"We had the name of being the toughest regiment in the army. We was, too. 'Cause we had Old Abe to lead us. I can see him yet. His beak open, screaming so loud we'd hear him over the shells 'nd cannon firing, diving and flapping his wings in fury through the clouds of black smoke and flames 'nd bursting shells. After the battle was over, Old Abe'd swoop down and landed on one of the braves' shoulder. Didn't matter none to him which one, just so it was an Indian brave. Never would light on one of our shoulders, but he got so's he'd let some of us feed him. He loved mice, and we'd scour the fields between battles, searching for rodents to feed Old Abe.

"Old Abe had his freedom to forage for himself, but he never flew out of sight of the boys in blue. Yes, sir, he was one splendid bird. Wisconsin boys was all mighty proud of Old Abe."

We stayed for the fireworks that night. Gramma and I rode home with Cousin Jerry and his wife. Ma, Pa, Little Jim and Ingie squeezed in the buggy with Old Joe pulling it. Old Joe was my saddle horse as well as Ma's buggy horse. He was a rangy bay, slow now and past his prime, but safe and gentle, a good horse for Ma and she loved him. When I rode horseback I wanted to get there sometime and not astride a poky old nag.

Chapter 4

We drove ahead of Pa because he didn't want to make Old Joe hurry. Dawg came to meet us when we were still nearly a mile down the road. After he checked us out, he waited for Ma and Pa. I helped Pa unhitch and take the harness off Old Joe. Pa gave him a measure of oats before letting him out in the pasture. Later, we rubbed him down good.

"He's earned it," Pa said. "It's been a long, hard day for him. He isn't used to being harnessed all day like that."

Most of the time we walked because we were close, but sometimes I rode Old Joe to school with Little Jim up in front.

When I complained how slow Joe was, Pa just said, "He's safe. Someday you'll have your own horse. Just wait . . . , there's lots of time for that."

Dawg was sure happy we were home. It was the first time we'd all been gone for such a long time since he came to us. He ran circles, going first to one, then the other for petting and tongue licking. He'd tagged Ma in the house, and the first thing I knew he was there with Pa and me. He chased one of the cats up a tree, just to let us know he was on the job, I guess. He knew Pa didn't like him chasing the cats.

When Pa said, "Dawg. Was that necessary? Now get away from that tree," Dawg acted like he felt real foolish and tagged at Pa's heels right to the kitchen door. Then he took up his vigil.

Little Jim couldn't stop talking about the fireworks, the races, and the parade.

"Did you watch Cousin Jerry ride that horse?" he asked. "He sure sits up there big in that old saddle, just like General Washington did, I'll bet. Bet even General Grant couldn't do no better'n him, with the flags waving and the band playing and the horse prancing. Someday I'm going to have me a horse, and I'm gonna sit up there and hold a flag just like Jerry. Yessiree, I sure am."

Ma knew it was past his bedtime. "He's over tired. Let him talk himself to s—l—e—e—p," she said, spelling out the last word.

Pa carried him into his bed.

The next day, when Ingie was taking her nap, Gramma and Ma were busy in the house. Pa and I were in the field. Little Jim was supposed to be playing close to the house, but instead he ran to the pasture. He caught Old Joe and led him over to the stone fence and pulled and pushed until he'd edged the old horse up close to the rocks.

The fence was a couple feet wide on top with a barbed wire

28

strung along the top to keep the farm animals from climbing over. That old stone fence was full of life; grape vines and woodbine covered it in places, bushes and brambles grew through it, and numerous wild flowers took root along the base. Birds built their nests in the bushes, and small animals and snakes made their homes in the crevices between the rocks, or burrowed beneath it.

Jimmy tied Old Joe to one of the bushes that grew beside the fence, and hiked to the barn. Somehow he climbed up and managed to get the saddle off the peg, because Pa hung the saddles and harnesses up high. He dragged the saddle across the barnyard to the fence and somehow got the saddle on the horse and tried to tighten the cinch.

It was a good thing Old Joe was so patient. He just stood, ears drooping tiredly and occasionally stamping a foot while he switched his tail at the flies.

Little Jim made a flying leap for Old Joe's back. He slipped. There he clung, all sprawled out, caught in the barbed wire, with one foot twisted in the stirrup and the saddle slipping.

Dawg was there. Yelping and barking in short, excited cries, he dashed for the house. He scratched at the door and the side of the house and whined. When Ma came out he threw himself at her in a frenzy, nearly knocking her over. He whined and ran toward the pasture and back to Ma.

"He wants something," Ma called, and Gramma ran after Dawg, too.

"Oh, dear Lord," Ma cried when she saw Jimmy's predicament.

Gramma held him while Ma got Jimmy's foot out of the

stirrup, and they both worked at getting him untangled from the barbed wire. Jimmy had one deep cut besides many scratches and bruises. Gramma was good at doctoring, but this time she knew he needed expert care.

While they were carrying him to the house, she told Ma, "We'll have to call Dr. Martin. Rusty wire could be infected."

Gramma washed his cuts with a little carbolic acid in the water, and she and Ma bandaged him. When Doc came he looked closely at Jimmy's wounds, opened his bag and rolled up his sleeves.

"You did the right thing in cleaning out the cuts," he said.

He worked on Jimmy for better than an hour. As he picked up his bag and prepared to leave, he said, "That's a good dog you've got there. If it hadn't been for him, Jimmy could have lost his leg."

Little Jim limped for awhile, but soon he was all over the place, like always, except a little slower.

I had to admit, Dawg sure earned his keep. When I leaned over and hugged him he cleaned my face, and I let him. I never saw a dog with so much tongue, and so quick with it. I didn't mind his lapping my hands, even my feet when I had my shoes off, but I didn't go for that face washing, most times.

The weather stayed hot and dry. Dust hung on everything. Where we walked in the fields, little puffs like smoke rose from the parched earth. Dust devils were common. If there was a little wind, you'd see eight or ten real close together, picking up and circling, with dust, leaves, and chips in the spinning center.

"Watch 'em," Pa said. "That's like a small cyclone-—gives you a pretty good idea what a cyclone can do."

The air smelled of smoke and there was a haze across the sun.

"There's a big fire up north——lots of the pinery is burning. You can smell pine smoke. Some of this smoke is even coming down from Canada," Pa said. "We sure need a good rain; the whole country'll burn up if we don't get one soon."

"When we get it, it'll be a corker," Gramma said. "This kinda weather is a real weather breeder."

The road into our place was grassy ruts cut in the sod, but because it was so dry we could see clouds of dust approaching before we saw the rig coming. Dawg began to bark, running from the road to the house, making a real fuss.

"Gotta be strangers comin' for him to make that much ruckus, Pa said.

Through the haze, we could see it was a sort of wagon with a top over it. A huge man sat up front, driving a four—horse team of spanking grays. Another rig followed. It looked like a medicine man's wagon, lighter than the first and painted brightly in red, blue, green, and yellow. It was pulled by a team of matched buckskins, dainty and high—stepping. There was a lady driving, and she pulled up right beside the larger wagon.

Dawg was carrying on something fierce. The hair on his neck stood straight up and he kept growling and baring his teeth.

Pa said, "Put that dog in the barn and lock the door."

I grabbed him and he pulled for dear life, trying to get away.

Gramma called from the kitchen door, "John, bring the dog here. I'll take care of him."

Dawg was more willing to go to the house, and Gramma said, low, "They're Gypsies. Watch out———they'll steal us blind. Dawg hates them, that's easy to see. He'll keep them away from the house. Get Little Jim in here, too. He and Ingie're better off here with me. Sometimes Gypsies steal little children."

I looked. More people were crawling out of those two wagons. The women had long black hair and flashing black eyes. They wore long skirts of red or orange or yellow, and low—neck blouses of different colors. Gold hoops hung from their ears. Their arms jingled with bracelets and gold chains, and around their necks were long strings of beads and more gold chains.

The men were dark and swarthy, bare to their waists, and the muscles stood out on their arms in bunches.

There were three women and three men, and one old white haired man wearing a red shirt. One of the women was carrying a baby wrapped up in a yellow shawl. Two little girls jumped down from the back of the wagon. They, too, had black eyes and long black hair, and they wore long red skirts like the women, but no blouses.

A boy, younger than I, got out of the first wagon and walked back to the second one. He, too, was bare to the waist like the men, but he was barefoot.

I thought I'd never seen such pretty women with their sparkling eyes, their bright flouncy skirts and glittering jewelry. One of them ran up on the stoop.

"Tell your fortune, lady . . . cross my palm with silver."

She spoke with an accent, hard for me to understand. Dawg was growling softly, rumbling deep in his throat.

Gramma held Dawg back. "No, I don't want my fortune told," she said, "but if you want to sit over there on the grass in the shade, we'll bring you all the milk and bread you want."

"Water?" the woman asked.

"Oh, of course," Ma said. "Here's a dipper." She pointed to the well. "Help yourself——anyone who's thirsty. Such a hot, dusty day."

Pa said, "If your horses need water, take 'em down to the creek. We're watering our stock down there these days, not enough wind to turn the windmill and keep the tank full for the stock."

One of the men and the boy unhitched the horses and took them down to drink. In the meantime, Ma and Gramma brought out plates of bread and butter and a big stone pitcher of cold milk.

"When that's finished, we'll bring more."

Ma had dried apples for winter, all strung on a string. She brought out a string of apples.

"Something for the children to chew on," she offered.

One of the women spoke up. "Not eat now. We take home to treat the others."

Ma passed apples she hadn't dried yet, and they ate them all, even the cores. Dawg stood on the stoop, still growling once in a while, guarding the house.

Gramma said, "You stay right there," and he did.

The Gypsies were camped in a big woods on the other side of town. They had been camped there a couple of weeks and would like to move on, but it was so dry they wanted to wait until after a rain. Many creeks were dried up, and they needed to be near water when they made camp-—with all the horses and people in their band.

The boy left the group and slipped around the corner of the chicken house.

The old man called, "No, Roman. Come here."

When the boy came and stood in front of him, the old man said, "These people treat us like brothers. Here we trade, no take."

They all nodded in agreement.

Year after year, that band of Gypsies returned, and we never had to worry about them stealing, but in town it was a different story. They were in and out of the houses like shadows; and in the stores, even though the owners were on guard and watchful, items came up missing.

Pa and the men were standing by the two teams of gray Percherons, carrying on an earnest conversation. Ma and Gramma had kept me busy carrying food, but at last I managed to slip over beside Pa.

He was saying, "I'd sure like that team of Percherons, but I haven't any money. They'd be good and strong to work in the woods. I'd make more money with a team of horses than I do with a team of oxen."

Pa ended up with the team of grays; he named them Mac and Molly instead of Macedonia and Magdalene. The Gypsies got Daisy, our young heifer due to freshen, ten chickens, some eggs and potatoes and several bags of corn, oats, and wheat. Ma threw in a big bag of Wealthy apples.

Pa was happy with the deal. Gramma didn't trust Gypsies.

"There's probably something the matter with those horses or they wouldn't get rid of them," she said. "Skinny as they are, probably got bots or worms. They're so poor, their ribs are sticking out like a bone covered with a hank of hair."

Pa said, "There's nothing much wrong with that team. They are so poor because with all the dry weather the pastures are burned up and brown. If they've got worms, I'll just add some fine—cut tobacco in their feed. Ten days'll take care of that.

"The Gypsies are short of feed, that's why they let one team go. I looked in their mouths. These are young horses, I could tell by their teeth. The other team was older. I could have my pick. Right now no one is buying horses 'cause they'd have to feed them all winter. Come spring, there'll be a good market for horse flesh again, when the spring work comes on. Won't take long, a measure of oats a couple times a day and Mac 'nd Molly'll show us." He patted the horses affectionately. Pa loved horses.

Before the Gypsies left the old man came to Ma. He held her hand and brought it to his lips.

"Bless you, my lady, and all that come and go under this roof."

"Why, thank you," Ma said.

He added, "A Romany curse is a thing to fear, but a Romany blessing is a thing to cherish. Our blessings are given to very few, our curses to many."

Dawg sniffed those horses over good. Once he made up his mind they belonged, he watched out for them like he did for everything else on the premises.

Chapter 5

"There isn't much flour left in the barrel,' Ma said, and she sort of walked it out of the pantry.

Pa jumped up to help her. Together they moved it into the hail, at the foot of the stairs.

"We'll leave it here," Pa said. "It'll be easier to get at here than in that dark pantry. I'll take the wheat to the grist mill soon. This afternoon or tomorrow for sure. How much flour you figure we'll need for winter?"

"That's what's left of six barrels you had ground last fall. The boys are getting bigger, and Gramma's with us all year now——at least one more barrel, I'd say," Ma answered.

She continued. "We can't keep too much on hand, after

winter it'll get weevily. We can't hold it over for another winter under any circumstances."

Gramma spoke up. "You've got a good dry place to store it. Seems like maybe two more barrels would be a good idea. Grandpa always said, 'It's better to be safe than sorry, "and you'll sure enough be sorry if you run out come spring. John here eats as much as a man, these days."

"Maybe you're right," Pa said, "but that pantry'll be mighty tight."

Ma said, "Couldn't you stack them on top of each other? That'd take a lot less space, and when I need a fresh barrel Johnny is big enough now so he and I can switch barrels when I need a fresh one."

"Good idea. Why didn't I think of that?" Pa laughed. "What in Sam Hill would I do without my little woman?"

The day was hot and muggy, but the sky was overcast.

"Thank goodness the sun isn't out," Ma said. "We'd all expire, hot as it is."

Everyone was in a good mood, hoping for rain.

Gramma said, "When it does come it'll be a jim—dandy, but I don't think we'll get it today. This is just a weather—breeder. I've seen lots of days like this in my time. Watch out for tonight, or tomorrow, maybe."

On the strength of her predictions, Pa harnessed up the grays. He and I loaded the wagon with grain.

"Even if we can't get it ground today, we'll leave the grain and go pick up the flour tomorrow. The trip takes lots less time with horses."

Pa was sure proud and happy with that team, and he couldn't

help comparing how much faster the work got done. He'd never think of making two trips to the mill with the ox team.

We had a flour mill several miles away in a place we called Springvale. It was always cool and green there, and several springs flowed together to form a fast, noisy stream.

The mill was an old stone building beside the stream. The stream was dammed up a little way back, and the flume ran right under part of the mill. There were wide cracks in the floorboards over the flume, and the water underneath was dark and black; it looked as though it didn't move it was so still and deep.

The miller was fat and jolly; his clothes were white with the flour dust, and his round red cheeks, his eyebrows and the black curly hair that showed under his cap were powdered white. He looked the way a miller should look.

His name was Johnny, and when I was little and we went to parties where everyone got into the games and played Happy Johnny Miller, I thought we were singing about him.

"Sorry I can't grind your grist today," he told Pa. "I had some trouble and had to build a new shaft… meant taking the big wheel out. It put me behind two, three days. But day after tomorrow I can have your flour ready for you."

It was a long hot ride home behind those matched grays. They jogged along, and Pa slowed them to a walk.

"We've got plenty of time to get there before dark, and I don't want to overheat these horses," he said.

They were draft horses, heavy and slow, but compared to the oxen, they moved!

I said, "Poor Old Joe can't go any faster'n this team, for all he's part Arabian."

Pa said, "Old Joe was a mighty fancy stepper in his day, but now it would be a crime to make him run fast. Your ma sets great store by him. He's been her horse since she was a little older than you are."

"He sure can run sometimes, when he's in the pasture, and kick his heels up, too."

"I guess he remembers how it used to be and tries to be frisky," Pa said. "But he can't keep it up for more'n a couple rods. He's a good, safe horse to have around."

"Sure do wish I had a horse of my own," I said. "I'd take real good care of him."

"I know you would, son."

Then Pa and I talked about what it was like to work in the woods and get up at four o'clock in the morning, clean out the stalls and feed your animals, and then go in for breakfast. Nobody talked, except to ask someone to pass something, and meals were over in fifteen minutes. Everyone worked till dark. After supper the men got together and sang and told stories, but not for long. Everyone went to bed early.

No one ever worked on Sunday, because something bad would happen if they did. Someone would most likely cut a foot or lose a finger or get his team hung up on a crossing. The men took baths, washed, and mended their clothes, wrote letters, played roughhouse games, sang and told stories on Sundays.

Some camps had bedbugs, or some logger came in with lice, and the whole camp would get them.

"That only happened to me once," Pa said. "I didn't get rid of 'em till I got home and Gramma fixed me up. You know how she's a great one for remedies. She made me wash my head with kerosene. The cure was 'bout as bad as the kill," he said with a smile. "I smelled of kerosene for a month. Couldn't get the stink out of my hair, no matter how many times I jumped in the creek and washed it every day." He laughed. "Good thing no one else in the family got those lice. Bugs was easier to get rid of. Your ma always makes me leave all my logging clothes outside in the air for a few days. The bugs'll crawl right away from those clothes, if there's any there."

We kept talking about the pinery and the shantyboys. The shantyboys were the workers who cut the trees, loaded the logs, broke the jams. The buildings weren't permanent structures. The cook shanty, bunkhouse and barns were built to house one special operation, and when that part of the woods was logged off, the crew moved to a different location. Pa figured he would go back to Fosterville, about fifty miles above Eagle River.

"From right here, John, as the crow flies, it's a couple hundred miles straight north of our farm. Fosterville is almost on the line between the two states, Wisconsin and Michigan. When you're logging it's hard to tell exactly where the line is. Sometimes you're cutting on one side, sometimes in the other state. The jacks call that cutting a round forty, when you're over the line, maybe taking timber that doesn't belong to you. The big companies don't much care… if the timber is good, cut it!

"It's all big pines up there. Lots of lakes, and sometimes in the spring some of the jacks go fishing. Cookie will fry fish up. You never tasted nothing better. Food is awful good in camp and lots of it———all you can eat in fifteen minutes. Nobody talks at meal time. It's shut up and eat. Cookie bangs on a pan and yells,

'Quiet!' There's pie and cake and doughnuts, and cookies, too, every day. All the meat and potatoes you can eat.

"We're up before daylight, and work till dark. Call us the 'hoot owl shift.' I figure with this team now, I should get about seventy dollars a month. Last year I got thirty dollars for me and thirty dollars for the oxen. I'm going to hit a couple of outfits and work for the company that pays the most penga. The work's the same anywhere in the woods, long hours and hard work. This is a good team. The lead team gets the best pay, and I'll hire out for that. Seventy bucks a month'll give me a good round sum to bring home."

Pa laughed when he explained some of the lingo the shantyboys used. "Everyone is a 'slave.''Chickadees' are men hired to sweep the manure off the iced roads. The roads are iced, so ice forms in the ruts——that way the road'll hold up all winter. Once that sleigh gets moving, it keeps moving. Every sleigh has to have good brakes, and the driver has an ox fork he uses to drive hay in the ruts, if we get going too fast for the horses.

"Fellers like me, farmers who work in the woods in the winter, are called 'pea pickers' and 'potato heisters.' Those lumberjacks have a name for everything and everybody ever worked in the woods. The man that keeps the roads in good shape is a 'road monkey,' some camps call him a 'blue jay.'"

Ma and Gramma were doing the chores when we got home. It was already dusk. I took a bucket of milk and started for the house while Pa took care of the horses. Ma was nearly finished milking, and Gramma went to make sure the door to the chicken yard fence was closed. When I opened the kitchen I could hear

Dawg, Little Jim, and Ingie; they were playing hide—and—seek upstairs.

The open staircase in the hall went upstairs. There was a bedroom on each side, and when I opened the hall door I could hear them running around up there in the bedrooms.

I yelled, "Hey, you kids. You know you aren't s'posed to be playing hide—and—seek up there. Ma doesn't want you to, and she'll be mad when she finds out."

"Is that so?" Little Jimmy hollered. "How's she goin' to find out? Big ci' tattletale. Who do you think you are, anyway? I don't have to mind you. Watch out!" and he made a flying leap for the bannister and came sliding down head first.

Pa had just come in and was standing right behind me. We both yelled at once.

I yelled, "Jim!"

Pa was yelling, "Hold it!"

Our words were too late. Head first, into the flour barrel Ma had set out of the pantry, went Little Jim.

There was one big poof—f! of flour. It flew all over the place. Jim's feet stuck out of the top of the barrel. His bellowing and blubbering were all muffled with his head in the bottom.

Dawg had come dashing down the steps just in time to get a face full. He tried to slam on his brakes and skidded halfway to the door on his rump, and that was all white, too, when he stood up. His red tongue hung out, dripping, and his eyes looked like two black holes burned in a blanket when Ma and Gramma burst into the hall.

Ingie, Pa, and I were dredged with flour. Dawg was barking

and Ingie was weeping, while Little Jim had begun to sound like Bankerts' bull bellowing.

Ma yelled, "What happened?"

Gramma never swore, but she took one look at us and screamed, "Mine Gott in Himmel! They're all crazy."

Jim was choking and sputtering, all muffled up. Pa grabbed him by the heels and dashed outside, slapping Jim's back as he ran. Jim started bawling his lungs out once his head was out of the flour. Tears rolled down his face.

Both Little Jim and Ingie kept crying, and their tears made a path of white sticky paste that stuck in their eyelashes and streaked their cheeks.

I never saw Ma so angry. She got the broom and tried to sweep us off. Then she got clean dry rags for us to wipe ourselves.

Little Jimmy kept snorting and snuffling. Ma and Gramma both thought he had flour in his windpipe and might choke. So Pa held Jim by the heels while Ma and Grarnma both pounded him on the back. Jimmy gagged and bawled and spit out a white sticky lump.

"There'smore yet," Gramma said, and Pa turned Jimmy upside down again and again.

Ma chased Dawg out of the house. Pa, Jimmy, and I had to go outside and take off our outside clothes and hang them on the clothes line.

After Ma washed Jimmy's hair he still had white lumps in it for nearly a week. Every night Ma took a fine—tooth comb and went through his hair while Jimmy sat and wailed. Dawg lay on the porch and whined, feeling sorry for Little Jim, I guess.

Ma would yank the comb through Jim's hair. "Let this be a lesson to you. You and Dawg both know better. Hide and go seek is for outside. You'd better remember that." Then she showed Jimmy all the pasty lumps she'd combed out, along with plenty of hair.

Jimmy bawled louder than ever and felt his head. "I'm gonna be ball—headed," he cried.

For once Ma didn't have any sympathy for him. "Serve you right," she snapped. "You mean bald—headed, don't you?"

Ma, Pa, Gramma, Little Jim, and I stayed up half that night, sweeping, dusting and sweeping all over again. Ma didn't dare use water on all that flour, and it was everywhere, thick and white and dusty. You'd be sure it was all cleaned up until what was stirred up cleaning settled again.

Ma had Pa dump the flour barrel. "We can't eat that stuff. Lord knows, I hate to waste anything, but that flour has got to go."

At last Ma called it quits for the night. The air was humid and close and not a breath of air stirring. Once in a while, sheet lightning flashed in the darkness; the heat was so oppressive it was hard to breathe.

Spot and Blackie were lowing softly, and Gramma knew.

"It's a weather—breeder, like I been telling you. You can even smell the sulphur in the air. It was the storm comin' made Jimmy do such a crazy thing. People do strange, wild things before a storm. Hear them cattle? They know what's coming."

It was so hot I thought I'd never be able to sleep that night. The next thing I knew, I was cold. The wind was blowing and rain was pelting my face. I heard the crashes of thunder and I saw the lightning flash as I closed my window. In spite of the storm, I slept like a log that night and I didn't come to until the next morning.

I had to laugh when I saw Dawg. He was covered with white streaks. Ma wouldn't let him in the house, he was so sticky and gummy from the rain and the flour in his fur.

Dawg acted like he was ashamed and went and hid behind the wood pile when I laughed. Pa called him and patted his head.

He told Little Jimmy, "Now you get that curry comb and clean that flour off'n Dawg's hide. It's your fault he looks like that, and it's your responsibility to clean him up."

After chores I helped Little Jim. Then we went to the creek, and Dawg went for a swim and got most of the flour off. The water in our creek was way high. Pa warned us all to stay away from there. "That current is mighty strong, and the water's getting higher. Don't go near the bank because you never can tell with so much water . . . part of the bank could break off. Just stay away."

The storm had been worse in some places. It had rained so hard one of the bridges washed out that we had to cross to get to the mill. Pa couldn't take the team and drive to the mill.

Ma wasn't able to bake bread because she didn't have flour. Finally, after almost a week and the bridge wasn't fixed, Pa saddled Old Joe. Ma gave him a clean flour sack and Pa said he'd try to get to the mill and bring home the bag full of flour.

Pa was able to cross the stream where it flattened out and was fairly shallow. He came riding home with the sack of flour across his shoulders. The water was still high. Pa was afraid if he put the flour bag on Old Joe's shoulders it might get wet, or splashed. Pa wasn't very impressed with wet flour.

The men couldn't work on the new bridge because of the

high water. Just two weeks before Pa planned to leave for the pinery, the bridge was fixed, temporarily. He went and got our flour for the year, and it was all stacked in the pantry, snug and dry, before he left.

Chapter 6

The time was fast approaching when Pa would leave for the pinery. Since the rain, the air was fresh and crisp, and the smell of smoke that had plagued our nostrils and watered our eyes was replaced by the smell of freshly cut hay that Pa was mowing and storing in the hay mow.

"There'll be plenty of hay for the animals' winter feed," Pa said. "All you'll have to do is bring in straw for bedding and grain from the granary. They're both close enough to the barn so you shouldn't have much trouble, even if the snow gets pretty deep."

Between the haying and getting up the winter wood, Pa and I kept busy. Pa used Timothy, the off ox of the team, to snake the logs out of the woods. When he had a big pile next to the house, he'd holler for help. Then Ma or I would take one end of the crosscut and Pa'd take the other. Some of the wood was sawed in chunks the right length for the kitchen stove, and some was longer for the other stove that heated the house.

Nights, after supper, Pa and I'd work on the wood. One of us would split and the other would pile the wood in the woodshed. Sometimes we all piled wood. Ma, Gramma, Jimmy, and Ingie, too, would carry small pieces.

The wood for the big potbellied stove that sat in the central part of the house didn't have to be split. The big chunks held fire better. If the fire did go out, we'd need small pieces of kindling to start it. After the first of November that old potbelly just kept going steady, days and nights. The stove pipe ran through the ceiling and up through Little Jim's and my room, to a chimney hole pretty high on the wall.

On cold nights we hugged close to that stove pipe while we undressed, toasting ourselves first in front and then in back. Then one of us would count one, two, three, and we'd make a flying leap for the bed and hunker down under the covers with only our noses sticking out. Once the quilts got warmed up we were warm and cozy, but it sure was b—r—r—rry! at first.

We piled some of the split wood under the stoop roof, close by the kitchen door. It was hard to hold fire overnight in the kitchen range because the wood had to be quite fine. Ma's kindling was in the small woodbox right near the stove. Pa always cut a few cedars, and he split it real fine for starting fires. Pancake wood, Gramma called it. It made a quick hot fire and and got the griddle hot in a hurry.

We had a big woodbox in the kitchen and another in the sitting room. Every night we filled those woodboxes when we came home from school, and made sure the small one had enough dry kindling.

School had started. Later we'd have a week or ten days of

potato-digging vacation. We never knew exactly when that vacation would be; when the weather was right and most folks were ready to dig potatoes, by mutual agreement, we'd have potato—digging vacation. When the potatoes were picked, vacation was over.

Pa did the digging and everyone in the family picked potatoes. It was my job to hitch Tom, the big black and white ox, on the stone boat, and haul the empty boxes down the rows and pick up the full boxes and haul them to the cellar.

The potatoes we were selling went in the double wagon box. When it was full we stored the extra potatoes in the granary until Pa could haul them to the potato warehouse in town.

Pa got way ahead of us with his digging, and instead of coming back and helping us pick as he usually did, he told me, "Carry on here. We've got to get these all under cover before nightfall. I'll be back in an hour or so."

He strode off cross—lots toward Grandpa's old place.

Little Jimmy was sick of picking potatoes and he yelled, "Pa. Pa! Wait for me, Pa. I want to go with you."

Pa paid him no mind, and Jimmy began to bawl.

Ma said, "Pa's got business to tend to, and so have you. Now get busy or we'll be here after dark."

Jimmy hopped up and down and squalled louder than ever.

I said, "He's a spoiled little brat, Ma. Why not give him what he's askin' for?"

Jimmy picked up a couple of potatoes and flung them at me. One of the spuds went whirling past my left ear, but the other hit Tom.

Tom started up on the run, and I yelled, "Now look't what you've gone and done! Whoa, Tom. Whoa, boy," and I ran as fast as I could.

I don't know where Dawg had been, but there Dawg was, right in front of Tom, running back and forth in front of him, making him stop before he wrecked the stone boat and dumped all the potato boxes.

When I had time to look around, Little Jim was back at work. I tell you, the potatoes were really flying in his box.

I was hauling the last load of potatoes to the granary when Ma said, "Gramma and I are going in and fix supper now, but Little Jim can come and get me if you need help."

She sort of loitered, not quick—stepping like she usually did when there were things to do. Gramma walked mighty slow, too.

Little Jim yelled, "Someone's acomin'. Ridin' a horse."

I looked down the road. "Why, it's Pa. He's riding Lady."

"How come you're riding Lady, Pa?" I asked. I stood up straight to take a good look at her. "She sure is a pretty little filly."

Pa rode right up beside me, and I took Lady by the bridle, petting her. She nuzzled me and rubbed her face on my arm.

"Ladybug, Ladybug," I murmured. "You pretty thing, you. I'd sure like to ride you."

Pa took his time dismounting, then walked around in front of that little mare and handed me the reins. "Here, son."

I guess I looked pretty dumbfounded. I didn't think anyone heard me murmuring to that horse.

Pa said again, "Here, son." He pushed the reins in my hands. "She's all yours."

Mine! I couldn't believe my ears. Mine? It couldn't be. That beautiful little mare was mine, that gentle little filly?

"Oh, Pa," I cried. "You don't mean it! You do mean it?"

"Hop up, son. Take her for a ride," Pa said. "I'll take care of the potatoes, and I'll feed good old Tom here. Take yourself a nice ride. Get used to her. She's a real lady," and he slapped Lady's withers.

What a horse this was. She rode like a rocking chair, such an easy, free gait she had. She ran, she galloped, she pranced. I guess she understood every word Pa said and she was showing me what she could do. When I said, "Show me a little speed, Lady," she hunched down and took long, running strides, faster than a racehorse. When I even whispered, "Let's slow down a little," she slowed to a quick running walk, her mane and tail flowing with the wind.

That night after Lady was rubbed down and fed and safe and sound in the big stall in the barn, Pa and Ma and Gramma explained.

"Your grandpa wanted you to have Lady. He said she'd make just the right horse for a boy's first very own horse. But he thought you should be a little older, he wanted you to be responsible. He wanted to be sure you'd take good care of your horse, and never forget to rub her down after a ride, and be sure she got enough exercise . . . never take chances that could hurt you or your horse. Grandpa figured at least fourteen before you had your own horse, and you're only thirteen."

"Right after the Fourth, your ma and I and Gramma talked about your having Lady this year. Your Gramma said, 'If he's going to be the man of the house, he'd better have a man's horse.'"

I was all choked up. "Oh, Pa! Ma! Gramma!" was all I could get out, and we hugged each other tight.

I had a horse of my own!

Chapter 7

I shivered in the chill dawn that brisk October morning, and pulled my jacket a little closer. It wasn't just the "frost on the punkin," as Pa put it, it was the sudden shaft of realization. Pa was leaving. Pa was leaving for the pinery now, in less than an hour. I would be in charge. Could I do it? I didn't know. I just didn't know.

I felt cold and alone, and frightened in a way I'd never felt fright before.

Pa hugged me close, and as if reading my mind he said, "John, my boy, you know I'm depending on you to watch out for your ma 'nd grandma and the two young'uns. You'll have to be the man of the house this year." He smiled and patted me on the back. "John, I know I can depend on you. If I didn't know that, I wouldn't be going. Understand?"

"I sure do, Pa." I gulped, and somehow I felt better. Pa's confidence in me gave me confidence.

Pa shook hands and gave my hand a hard squeeze and hugged me tight. He kissed Ma, special like.

"Oh, Mary, I'm going to miss you."

Then he kissed Gramma, Little Jimmy, and Ingie. "Good—bye now! You all take care, and the good Lord willing, I'll see you in the spring. When you write send it to Fosterville. Mail goes in to Mercer and the mailman brings it to the camps and towns. If I knew for sure what outfit I'd be working, you could send it there. Soon's I know, I'll write and let you know." We stood, clustered together for comfort, and watched Pa's rig until it was just a speck in the distance. Dawg had followed a little way, but Pa had sent him back, and he, too, pushed close to us.

Ma had packed Pa a big lunch. I'd filled the wagon box with hay and the feed box with oats for the horses. Gramma and Ingie packed a bucket of eggs in oats, so they wouldn't break, and Little Jim had carried armfuls of good dry kindling and put them under the high wagon seat.

Pa would be camping along the way. He'd sleep on top of the hay, besides using it for horse feed. He took a big piece of canvas along, and if it rained he'd spread it over the wagon box and crawl under.

"No need to worry about your pa," Gramma said. "He's been doing this lots of times before. Besides, he's got a slab of bacon, a bucket of fresh eggs, and six loaves of bread, 'sides the lunch your ma packed. And Ingie and I packed a tin box of m'lasses cookies. Now, we'd better get moving. Chores won't wait, and they got to be done before you and Jimmy take off for school."

Little Jimmy and I were in school all day, but sometimes in

the morning and every night I took Lady for a long ride, after chores. Sometimes Little Jim or Ingie rode in front of me, and Dawg always followed, trotting contentedly alongside.

Ma would rather take the buggy and drive Old Joe into town, but once in a while she'd ride Lady.

I said, "I'd better start breaking Lady to pull the buggy."

Ma agreed. "It would take a lot less time if I could drive Lady."

Ma, Gramma, and Ingie usually went to town once a week. Ma traded eggs and fresh—churned butter for sugar, salt, spices, or a length of material for an apron or a dress. It took almost all day because Ma just walked Old Joe all the way to the mercantile and back.

I started training Lady by getting her used to the harness and tugs, then I hitched her to the thills, fastened to a couple wide boards that dragged behind. Gradually I added weight on the boards. At last, one sunny Saturday, I hitched Lady to the buggy and drove her up and down the road.

When Ma saw how well Lady behaved she called, "C'mon, kids. Get your duds on and we'll all go to town. John can drive."

Everyone was happy but Dawg. He started to tag along, tail wagging and just barking happy little yips as he ran alongside the buggy. Gramma sent him home.

"You've got to watch the place, Dawg. There's no one home but you."

He stretched out on the stoop, head between his paws, and watched us go. He looked so forlorn, all alone, watching us with those sad, soft brown eyes.

I said, "You're a good dog, Dawg."

That cheered him up and his tail began to thump a little.

Ma, Gramma, and I sat on the seat. Ingie and Little Jim sat on the floor at our feet. I drove.

Ma only bought a spool of thread at the mercantile, and a little sack of candy with a couple peppermints for each of us.

Ma said, "Drive on through town. Gramma and I want to visit your great—aunts, Cynthia and Lottie. And mind your manners!"

Cynthia and Lottie were Grandpa's sisters, spinsters, who lived alone in a neat little house. They seemed much older than Gramma although they were of her generation.

"Ingaborg, now that Brother John is at rest, you should come and live with us. We've got plenty of room, and we'd love to have you. You're such good company."

Gramma laughed. "I'll think about it. Whenever you need some help all you need do is ask," she said when we were ready to leave, after supper.

On the way home she told Ma, "I'll gladly go and visit a few days, but a week is plenty. Two is company, and three's a crowd, you know."

It was nearly dark when we reached home.

"The days are getting shorter——winter's on its way," Gramma said.

Dawg was delighted to see us. We hurried through our chores, and Dawg tagged at my heels.

"Want to sleep in our room?" I coaxed him as I was getting ready for bed.

We were all very tired from our long ride and day out. Dawg followed me upstairs, but when I got into bed he began to whine and pace back and forth. He wanted out. I had to get up and take him downstairs.

He slipped through the door and stretched full—length on the stoop. That was where he wanted to sleep. He wasn't satisfied to stay in at night; he was a "for sure watchdog," like Pa said.

Seems like I just closed my eyes when I heard Dawg. R—r-r—a-aa—rrrfff! He was barking, a high, hysterical bark, and scratching at the door in a frenzy.

I jumped out of bed.

"What is it? What's wrong, Dawg?" I opened the window.

Dawg would run a few steps in the yard, away from the stoop, like he wanted to see my window, and he barked as loud as he could. I thought there was some varmint out there or someone was trying to break in.

Then I smelled it. Smoke!

Dawg had my attention now and ran barking toward the barn. He would run a few steps, look back toward the house and stop and bark.

I could see it. Smoke was seeping through the cracks and enveloping the whole barn in a sort of haze. I panicked.

I yelled, "Ma! Gramma! Come quick! Fire! The barn's on fire! Fire! Fire! Everybody up. Help! Help!"

What'll I do? My mind ran in circles, and so did I. I couldn't find my pants, then I couldn't button them. I sat down on the bed to pull on my boots and thought, What would Pa do? I remembered Pa saying, "You're the man of the house this winter. I'm depending on you."

Some man, I thought, running around like a chicken with its head cut off. I told myself to calm down and think.

I'd wakened Little Jim with my yelling, and he was scared

stiff, looking out the window and crying. I said a prayer, Dear God help me now.

How would Pa act? I took time to pat Little Jim's head.

"Find your clothes and run down to Gramma."

I dashed downstairs but somehow, all of a sudden, I was calmer, and I kept asking myself, What would Pa do? How would Pa handle this?

Ma was dressed. "Gramma, watch the kids."

She and I ran for the barn. Yellow spurts of flame were breaking through the roof boards and licking along the top boards of the hay mow. We could smell the marshy grass smoke, like burning grass in the spring.

"Open the gate to the barnyard, and you chase the animals through when I get them out of the barn," I yelled. "Get them away from the barn!"

My mind was finally working. We both knew we couldn't save the barn. There were two big straw stacks in the barnyard; if they caught fire, the animals wouldn't be safe in the yard either.

With Dawg's help I got the cows out right away, but the oxen, Tom and Timothy, took their good—natured time, slow and ponderous. I grabbed an empty feed sack and beat at them, and Dawg nipped their heels.

The barn was filled with smoke. It was hard to breathe. I could hear Lady and Old Joe in the horses' part of the barn. Old Joe was neighing in terror, and both were kicking and striking at their stalls, trying to get loose.

I yelled to Ma, "I'm bringing the horses out from the other side!"

The horses were tied to their mangers. Lady'd move faster, I thought, so I grabbed Lady's strap, and although she reared and snorted she let me lead her out. Ma came to meet me and grabbed Lady's strap while I went in for Old Joe.

Joe was wild—eyed and like a crazy horse from the smoke and flaming spears of hay sifting down from above. I still had the feed sack under my arm. I crawled in the manger in front of him while I managed to pull the sack over his head. I took a short hold on his halter strap and led him out of the barn to Ma.

"I'm going in to save the harnesses and saddle," I shouted as I ran back.

I had them out when I remembered Grandpa's Civil War saddle was in the far corner of the box stall. That barn was extremely dangerous now, filled with smoke, and even the straw bedding on the floor had patches of fire from the sparks falling from the ceiling.

What would Pa do? He'd say, "Don't take chances." I argued with myself. I can make it.

I ducked down low and sprinted through the smoke. I felt along the box stall and then heaved the saddle on my shoulders. Even as I ran, burned-through boards and big chunks of flaming hay landed in front of me. I reached the door and gulped a great mouthful of fresh air, and before me, looming like some war horse of old, came Old Joe. His nostrils flared, his eyes were glazed and steam seemed to spurt as he snorted.

Dear God, what do I do? With all my strength I raised up and flung the saddle from my shoulders in his face. From somewhere behind me Dawg burst ahead of me, and snarling and barking, he grabbed Old Joe by the nose and hung on. I ran clear, and Old Joe turned.

Immediately showers of sparks filled the night. The roof had fallen in. Only the timbers stood, outlined by the raging inferno within. The straw stacks were on fire, and like beacons of ages past, the flames shot in the air, sky—high.

Old Joe had been crazy with fear and he'd broken away from Ma. I'd heard of horses running back into a burning barn, and that had been Old Joe's intent.

We didn't have time to cry over spilled milk, as Gramma said. There was little wind, but a fire creates its own draft and that flying straw might start some other buildings on fire. The house was far enough away so we didn't need to worry, unless the wind changed. The chicken house, too, was out of range, and there wasn't much danger for the pigs. Their house was small and low, and I stationed Little Jim beside it with a bucket of water.

"If any sparks land on the roof, throw a dipper of water where it lands," I said.

The granary was a different story. The roof was high and peaked, and if that caught fire, there went all our feed. It was bad enough to lose the straw and all that hay in the barn, but we'd never make it through the winter without the grain.

I climbed on the roof, and Ma and Gramma carried buckets of water from the rain barrel. I soaked down the roof and I stayed there. As soon as a spark landed, I put it out, careful of how much water I used.

By the time first dawn appeared, we figured the danger of fire to the other buildings was over, and headed for the house.

Little Jim said, "I kept them old pigs' house from burning up. I just stayed right there, and when them sparks was flying I poured on more water."

Usually Little Jim's bragging got to me. I asked myself, What would Pa do? I patted him on the head.

"Good boy, Jim," I said. Then I had to laugh. Little Jim was black from hair to chin and his blue eyes sparkled like ripples on the creek when the sun shined, as he grabbed my arm.

"I did good, didn't I?"

"You sure did, kid."

That was the day I grew up.

Chapter 8

We were all "black—face" that morning. I took the buckets and went to the creek for water. Sometime during the day I'd have to fill Ma's rain barrel so she would have soft water for washing all our clothes, too, but right now we needed water to wash away the smoke and soot on us. Our well water was so hard it limed up the teakettle and coffee pot, and Ma's homemade soap wouldn't make suds.

Neither Little Jim nor I went to school that day. The next day Ma went to school and talked to Mr. Holmes. She brought work home for me, and at night she helped me so I could keep up with my class.

Mr. Holmes had said, "The actual experience John is getting at home, and the problems he has to cope with, are an education themselves."

We sat a long time at breakfast that morning after the fire

and talked and planned. We were all tired. The fire had started before midnight because Gramma looked at the kitchen clock when Ma and I ran for the barn. It was fifteen to eleven then, so we'd had only a couple hours' sleep.

"Wouldn't have made any difference if we'd stayed up later," Gramma said. "You couldn't have saved the barn no matter what. Spontaneous combustion like that and the fire shoots all over and lands in every corner."

I said, "Pa was sort of worried about the hay after that big rain, remember? But we turned those haycocks two more times before we put the hay in the barn. It should have been plenty dry."

"I can't believe Old Joe acting like such a crazy horse," Ma said. "Not like him at all. Oh, Johnny, you'll never know how I felt when he broke away from me and I saw him ready to run you down there in the barn door."

"He was wild with fear," Gramma said. "Horses do that, you know. Good thing Dawg was there. You know, Dawg was all over the place. Part of the time watching Ingie for me, down by little Jim, and helping your ma get those poky oxen out of the gate. He must've followed you in the barn, just before the roof caved in."

"Sure am glad he was there. Good ol' Dawg." I patted him and he just wobbled all over, he was so happy. Then I asked, "What had I better do about a place for the stock this winter? There's the two horses and two cows and Tom and Timothy to shelter, besides no straw for bedding, and our hay is gone."

Ma said soberly, "Chickens need straw, too, or they freeze their combs and won't lay."

We sat in silence, thinking. Then I asked, "Do you suppose I could add a lean—to on one side of the granary? I think I can get some straw and maybe hay, too, from Cousin Jerry. A lean—to would be plenty good enough for the cows 'nd oxen, so long's they get enough to eat and the wind can't hit 'em direct."

Gramma said, "There'd be room enough in Grandpa's barn for the horses, and I'm sure Jerry'd let us keep them there. But it's a long hike over there every time you need a horse."

Ma was thinking. "Johnny, if we move the grain all to one side in the granary, maybe we could fix up a couple stalls in there for the horses. They'd have to step up, but maybe you could rig up a ramp to the door. It'd be warm enough . . . , all that grain on one side and a lean—to on the other."

That sounded like a good idea, and we all went out to figure the easiest way to carry out our plan. The barn was now one big heap of ashes and smoke; the flames were gone, but that pile of glowing gray ashes would stay hot for days.

Ma and I and Little Jim went to work in the granary. We emptied two bins of grain which filled the remaining bins to overflowing, but by adding boards from the empty bins we could keep it contained. We emptied the bins closest to the door, and there were still a few extra boards which I used for the ramp.

Those two empty bins made like one big box stall, and with Lady and Old Joe together, we would need less straw. I made a sort of manger against the wall, and then Ma and I hitched Lady to the buggy (which had been left outside). Since it was so late when we got home I hadn't put the buggy away in its usual place at one end of the barn, so it was saved.

We drove over to see Cousin Jerry. When he heard what happened he and Cousin Lizzie couldn't get over how lucky we were, being able to save the stock and none of the other buildings catching fire.

"Lucky isn't the word for it," I grumbled a little. "We've got no straw, no hay, and I've got to get some sort of shelter for the cows and oxen."

The four of us walked together to the edge of the yard.

Jerry pointed. "Look at those two stacks, close to the railroad tracks. That's last year's straw, but if you pull away the outside it's nice and bright and sweet inside. You can hitch up the oxen and haul it for bedding. It won't cost you nothing——I was planning to burn it once snow gets on the ground because I want it out of there. I've been afraid some tramp might hop off a freight and sleep in it. If he started a fire, and the wind was right, everything I own could go up in smoke in dry weather.

"Down next to the marsh I got a couple stacks of marsh hay. The ground is froze hard enough now so's you can get to it. Marsh hay ain't the best feed, but it'll do in, a pinch. When I go to town I'll ask around. Could be somebody will have clover to spare, then you can mix the two. The animals'll get by, 'specially when you got grain for 'em."

He added, "You know, Liz, I smelled smoke this morning when I stepped outside. Remember, I said, 'There's a fire somewhere, ' but I figgered it was a ways off. I said, 'Smells like a marsh burning, so it's quite a ways off.' Never dreamed it could be so close--we couldn't see no flames. Last night we went to bed early, and it's cold enough this time of year so's the windows were closed. You was mighty lucky, I'd say. Lucky nobody was hurt 'nd you didn't lose any stock."

As we left, Jerry called, "I'll be over there tomorrow and give you a hand with the lean—to. I'll scrounge up any loose boards I can find and bring them along, too. Don't worry, we'll be all shipshape before the snow flies." He squinted at the sky. "Could be any day now."

As soon as we got home, I hitched Tom and Timothy to the ox cart. Ma helped, and we started hauling straw. Jerry was right, that straw was bright and shiny once the outside weathered layer was peeled away.

The next day Jerry and I finished the lean—to. We even built a manger for the cattle.

"This way, you won't lose any grain when you feed," Jerry said.

Ma helped me haul straw which we piled against the lean—to. We sure were busy that week and really tired out by nightfall, but it was worth it. It made a nice, warm place for the cattle. The granary was one wall; we'd built a back and a side, and the one end was open. There was so much straw, we piled that open end full, too, and left just enough room for one critter or one person to walk through.

The days turned cold and gray, and the gray sky spit snow in the air. Ma and I'd haul first a load of hay from the marsh, then we'd haul straw. Before the snow came to stay we had both straw stacks and the haystack moved.

I was back in school, and one noon hour Mr. Holmes asked me to stay after school a few minutes that night.

"Is it all right if Little Jim stays, too?" I asked.

Little Jim and I were really hitting it off these days, and I kinda hated to see him have to go on by himself, alone. I guess, maybe, once I began asking myself, What would Pa do? Made the difference.

"Sure, Little Jim can play on the swings till we're through talking," Mr. Holmes said.

After school Mr. Holmes asked, "Did you know they're fixing the bridge across the creek this side of Springvale, where it washed out in the big rain?"

I didn't know about it, but of course I knew about the bridge being washed out.

"I'm told they can use all the help they can get," he said. "I got to thinking, maybe you could rent out your team of oxen. It'd be a little extra money and you wouldn't have to feed them while they're working. Tomorrow's Saturday. The big boss is Jason Peters. If you think that's a good idea, go see him. He lives two places this side of the bridge."

I thanked him and hurried home to talk it over with Ma and Gramma.

"It would save a lot of feed," Gramma said.

"I wouldn't know what to ask," Ma said.

I answered, "Well, Pa gets a dollar a day for an ox team in the woods, and their feed. That gives us an idea of what to ask."

Ma and I drove Tom and Timothy to see Mr. Peters, and Little Jim was left in charge. You could just see his chest swell.

"Dawg and I'll look after everything. You bet. We'll take good care of Gramma and Ingie. We'll watch the place good."

Mr. Peters and I did some dickering. He wouldn't need the team all the time and he thought a dollar a day was pretty steep, but since we needed clover hay I could fill the cart and take it home. He would bring a couple more; he'd keep the team all winter and pay us fifteen dollars a month, and feed them good.

When I was looking at the hay I saw some traps hanging on a peg.

"Wolf traps," he said. "I used to do a lot of trapping, but now

I ain't got the time. You get five bucks bounty on a wolf and it ain't that hard catching them."

"Five dollars! Jimmy Crickets. That's something," I said. "Mr. Peters, you toss in them traps and show me how to set 'em and you've made a deal."

I was in business.

Chapter 9

Jason Peters was as good as his word. Not only did he sell me his traps, he took me out in the big woods between our farm and the mill at Springvale, and showed me his former trap line.

"I'm all done trapping," Jason said. "I used to do a lot of trapping when I was a young feller, but trapping ain't what it used to be hereabouts and furs ain't worth much these days." He entertained me with tales of his prowess as a beaver trapper while Wisconsin was still a territory. "I was a young buck then."

Muskrats were easy to trap and I knew how to catch them. The hides brought five, and sometimes, ten cents. Jason had a couple dozen rat and mink traps, twelve wolf traps and two bear traps.

I didn't want to do any bear trapping, but wolves brought a

five-dollar bounty, besides what the hide would bring. Anyway, even if the hide didn't sell, I wanted a wolf-skin cap.

Jason clapped me on the back when I told him about the cap and laughed. "I 'spect you want the tail, too. Lucky for you it's ears you turn in for bounty. Guess your cap won't need ears on it. I'll show you how to tan and treat the hide . . . if you get any skins."

"Oh, I'll get wolves," I said.

Jason just laughed. "They're plenty smart buggers."

Saturday morning, very early, I delivered Tom and Timothy to the Peters' farm. I'd tied Lady to the back of the cart, but those oxen moved so slow and poky, I took off her saddle and bridle and let her meander along the way. She'd come the minute I called her and didn't wander far from the cart.

Dawg wanted to come, too, but I made him stay home. Jason had said, "Don't take Dawg along when you're making your sets. He'll scare the animals way off in the next county."

It was nearly eight o'clock by the time we had the team unhitched and in the barnyard. Jason saddled one of his horses, and I jumped on Lady's back. We headed for the big woods.

I was so excited and so anxious to get those traps set, I almost forgot to take my bag of traps.

Jason said, "Now, boy, these traps are all ready to set. I boiled 'em in hemlock bark. Takes the man scent away and they look dark and discolored. They won't show up when you make your sets.

"Now, I'm taking you on the wolf run where I trapped. Wolves have a regular route they follow. It takes about three weeks for them to complete the cycle. So, we set your traps today——maybe you won't catch a wolf for two, three weeks, but you keep checking your traps every day. A wolf, coyote, fox, rat, almost any animal, will chew his foot off if he's left in the trap too long. I always believe, don't leave any animal in the trap to suffer and starve. Besides, you lose 'em! You make sure you check your traps every day."

Jason showed me the trail the wolves followed from his side of the big woods.

"This is where I set my traps, but it's too far away for you. We'll pick up the trail the other side of the woods, close to your pa's farm.

"Now mind. You check those traps, mornings, before school. Don't you get caught in the woods come dark. Now winter's here, it gets dark mighty early. Them wolves run in packs, and a wolf pack ain't nothing for a young feller to get mixed up with. A wolf usually won't come near you, but if they're hungry and hunting's poor, and they're in a pack of six or more, they might attack——especially if you're alone."

"What do you think about Dawg coming along when I check my traps?"

"Good idea. Once you get your traps set, take him along. Dawg's smart enough to keep away from your sets, I hope."

Again he warned, "Don't get caught in here after dark. It's too easy to get lost. Besides, these wolves ain't nothing to monkey with in winter. Summers ain't bad, there's plenty of food then. If they get hungry, they'll grab a farmer's calf. Every now and then Bill Jones loses a lamb or two. Baby pigs, too.

The big woods, as we all called it, was a large tract of heavily wooded, unsettled land, lakes, and streams, with one great marsh within its confines. The area took in acres of high and hilly virgin forest. A seldom—used road, which was an old military trail, ran through it.

We followed the wolf run and crossed the road several times until we finally came out on our side of the big woods. Then we went back in to the left of the road, and Jason helped me set all my wolf traps.

"Now, be sure you get your bearings before you go in. Pick out a couple landmarks, and always go in the same place. I don't want you getting lost. And mind you, stay out of here when it begins to get dark."

I had reason to remember those words.

We were having Christmas vacation. Ma, Little Jim, and I went looking for a fairly small Christmas tree. After that we went to the marsh and picked cranberries.

"They'll look nice strung with popcorn to trim the tree. They're good for sauce, too," Ma said.

The time flew. Little Jim, Ma, Gramma, and Ingie were popping corn; we'd string that when I came back from my trap line. It was past two when I grabbed my gun and called Dawg. Usually I rode Lady, but I might see some prairie chickens on the way or even a wild turkey in the woods. That would be a nice treat for Christmas dinner. I'd probably get a squirrel or two for sure.

I did get a couple shots at prairie chickens. One was a clean kill, and Dawg located the wounded one, so I slipped them both in my pockets and hurried for my trap line.

It was a dark day, and rather late to be checking my traps. By four o'clock the sun would set on those short December days, but I figured I'd make it before dark. There was a light snow on the ground. A bank of clouds was clumped in the west, and we could get a good storm out of this.

I hurried and called Dawg away from a couple of gray squirrels he'd treed. Reluctantly he left them, chattering and sassy.

"No time for those squirrels today, boy. Anyway, we've got a couple of birds. They're better for Christmas dinner than those sassy old squirrels. We've got to hurry now, but we'll come back and get 'em another day," I said.

There was nothing in the first traps. I hurried on. Then I came to a trap that showed signs of a struggle.

"What's going on here?"

I looked at Dawg and he cocked his head. There was fur on the ground and a large rabbit's foot; the leaves and grasses were messed up and the brown earth was freshly turned over atop the snow.

I said, "Funny. A rabbit would never go for wolf bait. Where'd that foot come from? What's going on here?"

I looked all around. My trap was gone. I could see something had been dragged over the snow. There were blood signs on the overturned leaves and flattened grasses; in places, the bushes were knocked down flat.

Dawg and I followed that trail nearly a mile back in the

woods. Suddenly the hair on Dawg's back raised and a low growl rumbled in his throat. He dashed in front of me and stopped.

Right there, not six feet ahead, in a thicket of hazel brush, stood the biggest, meanest looking gray wolf I ever saw. His head was slightly down and pointed forward. The hackles on his back stood straight up, his lips drew back over yellowed fangs and his eyes gleamed green.

He was caught by the right front foot, and when I took a second look, his left hind foot was in a trap, too. How did such a thing happen? I didn't know. Neither did Jason when I told him about it.

"Show me," he'd said. He looked the signs over and came to a conclusion. "Must be he took after that rabbit and got caught by the front foot when he was eating and not paying attention. Maybe something came up and tried to steal it. After he got caught he pulled out the trap stake by pulling and rearing back. See here." He showed me the tracks and marks in the earth. "Must be, he backed right into that other trap. That's what held him there."

When I raised my gun, that old wolf was all fight, ready to leap for my throat. I got off one shot. Barn! That wolf just leaped in the air, held fast by the trap on his hind foot. Dawg started to dash in and I had a time keeping him back, so's I could get off my second shot.

Jason figured my first shot really killed the wolf, but that wolf was so crazed and stirred up from getting in both traps that he couldn't quit thrashing, even if he was more dead than alive.

By then it was dark in the woods. I took my knife and took

the ears for bounty, because when I tried to lift that dead wolf he was so heavy it would take me till late to drag him out and Ma would be worried sick.

I called, "C'mon, Dawg. We'll have to leave him till tomorrow, cause Ma'll worry as it is. We'll have to follow the old road out of here. It's too dark to find the path."

I talked to Dawg as I backtracked the area where we'd followed the wolf. "Where's the road, Dawg? We've got to find the road. I know we crossed it."

At last I found the narrow cleared area, and we followed the faint snow—filled ruts. Overhead a screech owl wailed. We heard other peculiar sounds, whistles, snarls, and hisses, whether from the owl or something else; and alongside the road orange eyes followed us, moving as we moved.

Dawg's hair rose on his back, but at my command he made no attempt to attack our pursuer, just growled deep and long in his throat. It was an eerie feeling, walking along that road with the snow crunching under my feet, and along at my right something keeping pace, silent, ghostly, with never a sound to betray its presence, just those glowing orange eyes in the brush. Dawg kept at my side but he rumbled constantly, deep voiced and threatening.

Jason thought it was probably a lynx that kept pace, his pads light and soft. He said, "Big cats'll do that. He probably smelled those two chickens you shot."

I was glad when we got to the edge of the woods. Whatever had followed us stayed in the woods.

It had begun to snow earlier, real fine flakes.

Gramma said, "This is the real thing. This snow will stay on. We've got to expect colder days and plenty of snow from now on. Days'll be getting longer. When the days begin to lengthen, the cold begins to strengthen, you know."

The day before Christmas I saddled Lady and I took Little Jim with me, Christmas shopping. I had five dollars coming from that wolf I'd caught. We collected the bounty money and went to the mercantile.

I got Gramma, Ma, and Ingie each a piece of material, enough to make a dress, and a piece of pink ribbon for Ingie's hair. Little Jim helped me pick it out, and a purple brooch for Gramma that matched the print in the cloth I'd bought. We picked out a comb for Ma's hair, and while he was busy looking at the candy counter, I bought Little Jim a shiny tin whistle. He was always after Pa and me to make willow whistles, but they didn't last long. He just loved whistles. Then I bought me a knife. Jason said I needed a better one when I'd skinned out that wolf I caught. He said he'd show me some tricks about skinning with a better knife. I bought one for Pa, too. Even if he wasn't home for Christmas, I'd give it to him when he came home.

We had a nice Christmas. We opened our presents the first thing Christmas morning. There were warm mittens and caps for all of us from Gramma. Ma knitted Gramma a warm blue shawl, and Gramma had knitted Ma a soft brown sweater with a big collar and big pockets. Little Jimmy and I each had a red sweater from Ma; Ingie's sweater was blue, like Gramma's shawl. Little Jim liked his whistle so well, he even took it to bed with him that night. The next day I gave Jimmy my old knife. He sure thought he was grown up after that.

Ma roasted the prairie chickens for Christmas dinner, and for a surprise Mrs. Peters had made a big plum pudding and sent it with Jason when he'd come to help me skin the wolf.

Gramma read the Christmas story from the Bible after dinner, then we sang songs and carols. It was a good Christmas, even if Pa wasn't home. We knew he was thinking about us, too.

Chapter 10

We had scads of snow that winter. I used some of it to bank around the house. Usually we banked the house with straw, but this year we needed all we'd hauled for the animals. The snow made good insulation and kept the wind out. I banked around the lean—to, also. When Ma and Gramma went there to milk, they said it was just as nice and warm as it ever was in the barn.

"We've had more than our share of cold, too," Gramma observed. "But now the sun is getting up there so high you can almost see the snow shrink."

Soon water was running all over the place, and Ma began preparations for making maple sugar.

"Spring is just around the corner. Cold nights and warm days'll make the sap run, and we've got to be ready," Gramma said.

Ma was making sure she'd be ready when the trees were.

Grandpa used to say, "Your ma and gramma wouldn't miss sugarin' time if they were sick abed and had two broken legs."

Saturday came, and Ma kept Little Jim and me busy carrying firewood from the wood pile to the sugar shed. Built so we wouldn't need to carry the sap far from the trees, the sugar shed was just a roof set on poles over a big stone fire pit. It was built in a spot where just a few trees needed to be cut, at the edge of the sugar bush.

There were iron bars across the top of the fire pit, and Ma had a couple large shallow pans that just about fit the top of the pit. When the sap started running, we poured the buckets of sap in the pan and kept a fire roaring while the sap boiled down to syrup.

R—r—r—a—aa—rrrfff! A—aa—rrrfff!

I stopped hauling wood and walked toward the house to see why Dawg was making such a fuss. He ran, barking furiously, and stood on the stoop. He'd look toward the big woods and then turn to the kitchen, as if he wanted Ma to come outside.

Ma opened the door, and the smell of bread baking wafted through the fresh spring air. Ma'd just come out of the dark kitchen into bright sunlight, and she peered toward the woods.

"John, do you see anything? I don't know what ails this animal," she said.

At first I couldn't see anything, and then I exclaimed, "Ma! There are people coming out of the woods. Can you see them? They're in the big field now, single file. Looks like they could be Indians." They were closer now. "Yup. They're Indians."

Ma could see them now. "There's five of them. Might be a hunting party," she said. "You and Little Jim better get inside, and you hang onto Dawg. Don't let him chase them."

"Jimmy, sit here, close to the stove, and keep still," Ma cautioned.

Gramma looked out the window. "Looks like a hunting party to me, too, but I don't think they got anything. I don't see any game."

Gramma had Ingie by the hand, and Ingie was hanging on for dear life, sort of peeking around Gramma's skirt. Gramma murmured, "Indians. Real live Indians. What're they doing here?"

I watched from the window. There were five Indians, just like Ma said, with feathers in their long black hair. Although the sun was shining, the wind was cold, and those Indians looked cold, huddled in their blankets. They were dressed alike, moccasins on their feet, blankets around their shoulders, and they all wore beaded headbands with feathers, except the first Indian at the head of the line had a single white feather. The others had gray feathers.

Arms folded across their chests, they stalked in through the door without knocking. Pointing to the oven, the brave with the white feather spoke in a husky voice. "Bread."

Ma always fed the hunting parties. She had a loaf of bread left from her earlier baking. She cut huge slices and carried them to the table where the Indians had seated themselves.

Dawg was straining to break away, snarling and growling deep in his throat. He made a frantic leap and almost wrenched away from me, pulling me with him closer to the table. One of the braves leaped to his feet and pulled a long hunting knife from his belt, menacing Dawg, knife in hand he raised his arm, but White Feather was faster. He grabbed that brave's arm and said something I didn't understand. With a sullen, mean look at Dawg and me, the brave put his knife back and slowly sat down.

Ma spoke sharply to Dawg. "You behave yourself now. Dawg, you keep quiet and stay down. Down, I said."

Dawg respected the authority in her voice, but he still rumbled, deep in his throat. He lay quietly. I kept a good firm grip on his collar, just in case.

Ma took the hot bread from the oven and cut it the best she could. When she placed it on the table it was still hot. She tapped White Feather's shoulder.

"Hot," she said, and made motions from the bread to the stove. "Hot," she repeated while going through the motions of blowing at the bread with her lips.

White Feather seemed to understand and spoke to the others.

The Indian with the knife grunted, grabbed the hot bread and stuffed his mouth. He yelled, jumped to his feet and raised his arm to Ma. Dawg went wild, and I was about ready to let him go.

Quick as a wink, Ma turned. She grabbed the hot poker with one hand and with the other she gave that big Indian a good hard push. She motioned for him to sit down and shut up. White Feather had jumped to his feet, but when he saw Ma could handle the situation he sat down and kept eating.

I never saw anything like the way those Indians could eat. I watched them tear into that bread like there was no tomorrow, and Ma just sliced loaf after loaf of bread. At last they rose from the table, and single file, marched out the door.

White Feather stopped in front of Ma. "Brave squaw," he said with a half smile.

The brave with the knife was last in line. Ma had one loaf of bread left. With a scowl, that Indian snatched the loaf and put it under his arm as he stalked out.

We watched them pass through the gate, mount their ponies, and ride off.

Ma said, "That young brave with the white feather is Chief Flying Eagle's son. He's been here before. Sometimes with his father, sometimes with other hunting parties. They always stop here. They're friendly, so are those two older Indians, but I never saw the one with the knife before."

"I thought Dawg would pull away from me for sure. It was all I could do to hold him."

"That was a mean old Indian that almost hitted Ma," Jimmy said. "I wish ol' Dawg'd got a hold of him. Old Dawg could fix him good. He sure would. He'd just bite that mean Indian all to pieces."

Ingie ran to Ma and clung to her skirt. "I don't like those mean mans. They eated all our bread," she said, and sighed woefully. "I'm hungry."

"Poor baby. Ma'll find something for you to eat. I guess it's time we all eat, after all the excitement."

Ma poured us milk; she sliced potatoes into her big black skillet and put eggs on to boil. "We'll have plenty to eat, even without any bread."

Gramma set the table. She was disgusted. "There wasn't any call for them to eat so much. Now you've got to start right in and set more bread. You'll be baking bread at midnight tonight. That thieving Indian took your last loaf or you could wait until tomorrow, even if it is Sunday."

Ma just laughed. "Gramma, if a few loaves of bread'll keep the Indians friendly, I'll gladly bake bread twice a day. We've always fed the hunting parties but Jim has always been home when they came before. This is the first time I was alone, without Big Jim. I've got to admit I was scared, shaking like a leaf."

"You didn't show it," Gramma said. "I felt my heart turn right over when you gave that snarly squint—eyed savage a shove. You sure surprised him, you did."

"He made me so mad, I didn't even think what I was doing," Ma said. "The hunting parties never caused trouble before. I can't say I'd want that one back here. He's a troublemaker, that's easy to see. Dawg didn't like him either. He'd have had that one by the neck if he'd had a chance."

"John, go in the store room and bring me some dried corn. That should taste good with fried potatoes. And while you're there bring some dried peaches, too."

We didn't miss bread with our meal and we made a joke of it, and laughed a lot. We'd had a real scare and were relieved to think it was over, so we "let our hair down," as Gramma said.

Ingie was so exhausted, she fell asleep at the table. Gramma picked her up and took her in the bedroom because Gramma and Ingie usually took naps together.

Dawg was snoozing under the table. Suddenly he leaped to his feet, nearly upsetting Gramma's empty chair. The hair on the back of his neck was raised and he was growling at the kitchen door, demanding to get outside. I opened the door, and Dawg made one flying leap from the stoop toward the lean-to, barking furiously.

"Ma, they're back," I yelled, and I made a flying leap from the stoop. "It's the Indians!"

Two Indians had let Spot out and were driving her toward the big woods, running after her with sticks. One turned around to face Dawg. That was a mistake. Dawg made a leap for his throat, struck his chest and knocked that Indian flat on the ground. Dawg just stood there, teeth bared, keeping that Indian flat on his back.

The buck with the knife ran for Dawg, ready to kill him. I knew I couldn't get there in time to save Dawg and I said a silent prayer. My gun was in the house. I was running for dear life. I leaned down, picked up a cobblestone, paused for just a minute and flung that stone with all my might. I was lucky. It hit the brave's knife arm, and his knife flew into a soft snowbank left from winter, and sank from sight.

I shouted to Ma, "You and Jim get Spot before she gets into the woods! Dawg and I'll take care of these bums."

That Indian came running at me and knocked me down in the mud. I twisted and turned. I tried every dirty trick I knew about fighting, but I couldn't shake him. I was fighting for my life. He had me by the throat, his long fingers squeezing my windpipe. I couldn't breathe but I kept struggling. I tried to think, and I clawed at his hands until I got one finger and bent it back, trying to loosen his grip. He just grunted and squeezed tighter.

I closed my eyes and went limp, thinking, If he thinks I'm dead, maybe he'll loosen his hold and I can away from those choking hands. He just choked me harder. My ears rang, my throat burned. This is it. I'm a gonner. I've had it.

They say at a time like this your life flashes in front of you. I just wished for Pa.

I gave one mighty shove, and his hold on my neck relaxed. Then faintly, like from a long ways away, I heard, "Get your hands off him! Just try fighting someone your own size, you miserable renegade. If he's dead, I'll shoot out your right eye first then I'll shoot out your left eye, you low—life, low—down scalawag! Get away from him!

"Johnny, Johnny boy, are you all right?"

I couldn't believe my ears, or my eyes. That was Gramma,

and she was hopping mad! She'd grabbed my gun from where it hung, and stood over us with the barrel pressed right against the brave's temple. She was going to use it if she had to. I'd never heard her use language like that before and I hardly knew it was her voice. It was a side of Gramma I didn't know. That Indian respected it——he knew she meant what she said.

Without the Indians to chase her, Spot had been turned back easy and Ma and Jimmy were in sight.

Gramma yelled, "Jimmy, you got your knife? Run and get the twine and see if you can tie this no—good thieving rascal up."

She was still mad. I could hear it in her voice. I was able to stand up and get my breath, but I was still too woozy to be any help.

Now that was something to see. Gramma held her gun on the Indian, and Jimmy took the ball of twine and tied that Indian's hands behind his back so tight and with so many knots he'd never get loose.

"That's it," Gramma said, "now his feet."

Jimmy cut the string and went for his feet. The Indian brought his foot back, ready to kick Jim in the face, but one look at Gramma was enough.

Oh, Little Jim knew how to tie people up, for sure. At school they played U.S. Marshals and bank robbers or scouts and Indians; someone was always late for the bell because they'd been tied too tight.

Everyone was busy watching Jimmy and the Indian. From where I was I thought I heard a rig approaching——and fast——or was it the ringing in my ears that sounded like thundering hoofs?

Little Jim was still tying up my Indian with Gramma and Ma watching, but Dawg was acting strange. Half wagging his tail, he was looking down the road one minute, snarling and threatening the Indian he had down the next, as if he knew something was up and didn't quite know what to do. I knew something was up, and then I saw.

"It's Pa," I yelled. "It's Pa! Pa's back. Pa's home!"

I felt like a little kid again. "Oh, Pa!" I ran into his arms and felt so comforted with his arm around my shoulders.

We were all terribly glad to see him, and we were all hugging each other when I remembered poor Dawg. Happy one minute, tail wagging, giving a happy little bark, he changed to rumbling deep in his throat, snarling at the Indian, never changing his stiff—legged stance.

It didn't take Pa long to get the picture.

"Tie this one up, too, Jimmy boy. We'll take him to Chief Flying Eagle along with the other one. They'll probably wish they'd never been born by the time he gets through with them. He'll handle them his way."

Pa shoved both Indians in the back of the wagon. Dawg was free now and could run up to Pa to be petted and praised with the rest of us.

The noise had wakened Ingie. She stood on the stoop for a minute then rushed into Pa's arms.

"Papa, Papa. You're home!" She cuddled under his chin, both arms tight around his neck.

We were all talking at once and didn't notice, until Dawg began to rumble, that White Feather and his two companions were riding into the yard.

Pa explained the situation.

White Feather said, "We missed these two and backtracked to see what was going on. We'll take them to my father. I was afraid they had done something when they didn't join us. That one is bad." He pointed to the Indian that had jumped me. "The other is just foolish, and will do foolish things when he's told to." White Feather yanked them out of the wagon; he wasn't gentle. "They'll walk to camp. No ride." We watched until they disappeared in the woods.

Dawg, too, kept quiet at Pa's feet. Pa reached down and patted him.

"Good old Dawg. Don't know what we'd do without you."

I agreed . . . he was some Dawg!